7 Sampler Series: Book 2

A Clearing

and 6 more spooky tales

Gavin Boyter

7 Sampler Series: Book 2: A Clearing

First published in 2023 in Great Britain by Sword Pen Press (an imprint of Gugnug Press, Edinburgh).

"A Clearing" was first published in The Periodical, Forlorn, and "Eyes in the Dark" appeared in Blueing the Blade.

Cover Design by Nivag Retyob

Set in Garamond (body text and footnotes) and Corbel Light (headers).

ISBN: 978-0-9571298-8-7

www.gavinboyter.com

For those in the throes of horripilation.

Contents

Acknowledgements

Thanks for their continued support, to my parents, sisters, brothers-in-law, nephews and niece. Many thanks are due to all the magazine, website and anthology editors who appreciated my work enough to publish it, or were kind in their rejections. Appreciation must be shown to the staff of the Foyles Café on Charing Cross Road, and Cliff's on Northdown Road in Margate for providing conducive spaces for writing and dreaming. Gratitude, as ever, to my London friends, especially Aradhna, Guy, Sara, Rob H and Indy, to whom I have read some of these stories or received authorly advice. Thanks to my new Margate friends too, for keeping me sane during the transition from the capital to the coast. Lastly, but not leastly, thanks to the London Writer's Café and Ramsgate Writers Unleashed for comradeship and helpful feedback. There will be more...

About this Book

The challenge of writing and selling short stories is that it's very much a niche format. In truth, few people read them, and short stories rarely, if ever, make anyone any money. The heyday of Amazing Stories, Reader's Digest and Harper's paying writers hundreds of pounds for a story has long passed. The golden age of the short story is sadly over.

Although there are fans who collect and enjoy short stories, most successful collections are published by previously bestselling authors trying their hand at the short form. They bring their fanbase with them, in other words.

That said, short story collections do allow writers and readers to explore multiple characters, narratives, locations and genres in one compact package. They offer a taster of the imaginative world of a particular writer (or a host of writers in themed collections) which can be immensely helpful when readers are trying to ascertain who to invest their time in.

Would you embark on a 1000-page novel by a writer whose work you've never sampled? That's a big ask of any reader.

Short story collections offer the security of the finite nature of the format. The short story, even in the supernatural genre, makes a bold promise: after a few thousand words, each tale will be resolved. Or at least, if not resolved exactly, then certainly *over*. The terror, the dread, the anguish will end (for readers and protagonists!)

I've put together this short, bargain basement sampler, as a way of letting readers dip their toes in the waters of my shortform work, for less than the price of a coffee.

This book is one of seven I will be releasing, which, should you collect the set, will allow you to read 49 of my stories for less than the price of a bowl of pasta.

This book has a broadly supernatural basis, but within that definition, there are a range of genres. Between these covers, you'll find M. R. Jamesian scholars, modern day ghost stories and uncanny tales. If you enjoy these stories, do turn to the back of the book for a list of the other titles in this series, and my other published works.

If you have fun with these spooky tales, you may find much to admire in my collection Running Coyote and Fallen Star, or my crime novel Elena in Exile.

But for now, find a comfortable nook where you can look out on a misty garden, or an eerily empty yard, and delve into a world between worlds…

(Margate, August, 2023)

A Clearing

Running saved me. It sounds hyperbolic but I wouldn't still be here, engaged in the banal act of assembling an Ikea bookcase (or avoiding doing so, if I'm honest), if it weren't for the simple act of putting one foot in front of another, at speed, through the English countryside.

When my marriage fell apart, it prompted a period of retrenchment and isolation. My wife and I had been gnawing away at one another for years, our arguments increasingly futile, repetitive, and vitriolic. She wanted me to be more decisive, to take more responsibility or, at the very least, to appreciate how much slack she picked up in our partnership. I wanted her to relax more, fret less, let go of past failures and accept that we will never achieve more than a fraction of our overweening ambition.

In effect, we were saying to one another "I wish you could be a different kind of person". There was of course, a ready solution to this intransigent dilemma - we split up and found other people. Diane met a young man whose online fabric retail business was booming in a way my career as a novelist clearly was not. I found someone else to spend quality time with - myself.

We sold the house and divided the proceeds, I took the campervan we rarely used, she kept the car. We went our separate ways, Diane to move immediately in with Masood, which I smugly knew was a mistake she'd greatly regret, me to a folly on the Kentish coast, a ramshackle barn I'd decided to renovate, whilst living in the van. I think the audacity of this decision is in part explained by my desire to show that I could have been the man of action and responsibility that Diane had always wanted, as if this would somehow prove a sweet revenge, rather than an onerous and expensive ordeal.

Nine months later, I'd project managed the three-hundred-year-old barn, which overlooked a ragged crescent of seashore, into a barely watertight bolt hole. Storms and seasons did what they could to reduce my ambitions to rubble but, watching my savings dwindle away to nothing, I finally moved into my new home as autumn began to give way to the inevitable chill of winter. Only the bathroom and one bedroom were complete but at least I didn't feel like a vagrant squatting in an unheated van at the edge of a building site. The workmen went about their days, nodding amiably to me as I went about mine - answering long-avoided emails and trying to plot out a new book.

One problem immediately presented itself. I'd successfully distracted myself from the depressing realities of my life but now that the house was becoming habitable, memory and regret moved in with me. They were not convivial housemates.

When I needed to escape the solitude and the seething tumult of memories and regrets, I'd go for a run, rediscovering an activity from my youth I'd long abandoned. I started with the occasional jog along the coastal path, adding a mile or two each week. My first run ended with me collapsing onto the pebbles covering the beach with lungs ablaze and heart thundering like a herd of rhinos. I coughed compulsively for over an hour - the detritus of eight years of juvenile smoking catching up with me. My bad habits ended with my marriage. Or perhaps I should say that new ones took their place.

From this first agonizing jog, I gradually built up my stamina until I could manage seven or eight miles in the space of an hour. Then, looking for variety, I discovered a drove path leading up into the hills and skirting a small patch of woodland I felt immediately drawn to. It had the evocative name of Weirwynd Wood and was evidently listed in the Domesday book (or so a helpful tourist information plaque informed me). A stile and finger post invited me in, and I clambered over and quickly lost myself in a crisscrossing network of paths and streams ribboning their way down the hillside to the sea below.

From the forest, the perpetual wash of surf was mixed with the rustling of the leaf canopy and the grace notes of birdsong, ceaseless and varied. On that first forest run, I could name very few of the birds that perched in the branches above me as I ran, but after just a few weeks I knew them by their melodies. They were my unseen companions and I even tried to mimic their music in a faltering whistle, to no great effect.

After six months, satisfied that my home was watertight and windowed and leaving the workmen to electrify, plaster and plumb, I began to take longer and longer morning runs. In part this was to get away from the incessant hammering and drilling, as well as the necessity of a small talk that didn't come naturally to me. The builders came from as far away as Latvia and Lesotho, but I didn't want to become their friend and couldn't abide their well-meaning but banal questions. So, I was a writer - wow. Where did I get my ideas? What was I working on now? Would I have written anything they'd know? I had answers for all of the above - from the junkyard of my memories, a middling, derivative thriller, and no, I have not - but I knew these would sound glib and dismissive and self-loathing. Instead of failing to connect, I absented myself.

I kid myself that these daily long runs were

building towards something - perhaps I'd enter a marathon or undertake some sort of adventure - running the coast of Britain, perhaps. I told myself that although I wasn't writing my book, and hadn't really worked effectively for weeks, my subconscious was laying the groundwork. Ideas were percolating, plot lines taking shape. In truth, I was running from the tyranny of a blank screen and avoiding my agent's calls.

As autumn gave way to winter, and the trees of the forest shed their crisped parchment leaves, I ran with memories gasping to catch up with me. The way Diane would spontaneously massage my shoulders after a long day at my desk. The window box garden I surprised her with when she returned from a business trip overseas. Drinking wine and listening to Joni Mitchell, making love in the attic in a nest of dusty old blankets.

One morning I tore open the mail, nodding a terse thank you to Keith, the local postman, as he wobbled away on his bike. Inside a crisp white A4 envelope was a sheaf of papers, signed and expensively letterheaded. Brickman, Lewis and Partners. *Decree Nisi.* So, this was it. I'd known it was coming - we'd decided not to wait for the formalities before disentangling our lives - but somehow seeing it in print made my knees weaken and my chest tighten with anxiety. I considered having a drink, but I'd always told myself that so long as I didn't start morning drinking, I was still a civilized member of the human race, no matter how attenuated my circumstances became. I laced up my running shoes, choosing the Saucony trail pair I'd just worn in. I had to run. Nothing else could take me away from the spiraling sadness beginning to fill me.

Almost angrily, I set off along the coastal path, ignoring puddles and patches of mud, reveling in the fact that I could just splash and slosh through them. It felt like a minor superpower at times, this ability to race through terrain hikers and dog walkers would pick their way around. I loved the fact that my legs were soon streaked with mud up to the knees. It didn't bother me that my feet were soaking wet. I wanted this run to be extreme, to take me to a place where the physical intensity of my movement obliterated the clamor my head.

I achieved this about four miles in, when pausing to gasp for breath at a familiar gate, I had to decide whether to turn back or head up the footpath to Weirwynd Wood. As I weighed the pros and cons, something cold and wet touched my cheek. For an absurd moment, I thought it might be a tear, until I realize that it was something rarer still - a snowflake. I looked up and a swirl of flakes was falling from a sky that had whitened without me noticing.

The weather made my decision for me - it would be wonderful to run in the forest in the snow. I climbed the fence and headed up the tussocky slope to my left, making for the gnarled nest of bare trees that decorated the hillside. As I got closer, breathing labored but refreshed by the newly icy air, the trees looked somehow forbidding and inviting at once - a challenge and a promise of the kind of intensity I was seeking.

As I squeezed through the narrow gap in the fence surrounding the wood, I saw that the snow had already salted the ground with a thin layer that was quickly accumulating, obscuring the chilled earth and moldering leaves beneath. Seasons don't so much supplant one another here as crossfade. The winter would preserve some of those autumn leaves well into spring and impetuous crocuses would start appearing through the frost on the sun-facing slopes in a matter of weeks.

I ran the now familiar outer loop of the forest, splashing through the streams and watching my breath gust out around me, as if I was generating the mist that was beginning to settle on the hillside. I dug into the forest, following my instinct and soon found myself in a region I'd not visited before, where the trees thinned out into a clearing at the top of a small rise. A horseshoe of oaks and maples faced me, a large, gnarly yew in the center, its corded trunk twisted into a profusion of branches. I slowed to a walk, catching my breath, emerging from my own cloud. I walked up to the yew and felt its ancient bark.

I'd read somewhere that yews are amongst our oldest trees. I guessed that this one might be hundreds, even thousands of years old. Carved into its thick bark were dozens of letters and dates. Carved initials, hearts and declarations. Josie 1975. B & L '22. Others that could no longer be deciphered - the decades had eradicated their promises.

Two letters were carved inside a near-perfect circle, decorated with diamond patterns. An E and an S. I guessed these were the initials of the artist but what he or she had meant by their handiwork, I couldn't guess. Perhaps simply to assert that "I was here" in an age before everyday identity was immortalized, fixed and copied endlessly in a digital realm. ES had no web presence, but he had this.

I took a swig from the bottle of water I carried with me, turned and ran back down the slope, taking a different route, with the intention of emerging on the high edge of the wood. But somehow, I found myself looping alongside an impenetrable hedge and back down, over a slope of tangled roots, then taking a sudden turn through a dense thicket and back into… the same clearing I'd just left.

I laughed at my error and decided to retrace my footsteps and leave Weirwynd the way I entered it. The snow was now lying two inches deep and making everything look different from how it had upon my arrival. Boughs dipped low with their burden and there were no footsteps to follow.

Nevertheless, I reversed the sequence of turns I'd taken to get here - left, right, right, left, over the fallen log and finally…. no, that's not right. I'd reached a fork in the pathway. I must have missed it on my way into the wood, but I now realized I had no idea which way to go. Just then a muffled sound could be heard, its source apparently some way down the left path - a girlish laugh, perhaps, although it had been brief. That decided it, I'd run that way and if I met a local, so much the better - he or she could redirect me if I'd gone astray.

I felt the first finger of a chill grip me - the sweat cooling against my skin. The thin jacket

I'd worn was now completely ineffectual against a rising wind that blew directly into my face, swirling flakes up my nostrils as I ran. I'd normally have enjoyed the extremity of it all, but something felt wrong, and not at all entertaining.

Surely I'd been running for far too long now. No more peals of laughter sounded, and I met nobody but it didn't matter - I should definitely have reached the edge of the woods by now. And yet, the gently curving path ahead of me, though encouragingly wide, seemed impossibly long. Had I somehow got turned round? Perhaps I should head back to that junction. My forehead felt cold and I could sense a headache coming on. Why had I chosen to wear a thin cap instead of a proper woolly hat? I turned and looked back, just in time to catch a hint of movement, a rustling in the underbrush.

"Hello?" I called, not expecting a reply from what was probably just a badger or fox.
The trail of my footprints was already filling in

with fresh snow. How quickly the world erases us, how indifferently our flickering lives register against the centuries, I thought, filing the phrase away for future use. I took a few long, icy breaths to calm myself and ran on. It didn't matter which way I was heading now. I had to keep moving. Something was gripping me - something familiar I hadn't felt since the drive south after the separation. I felt fear - a kind of grinding terror that everything which made sense was slipping away. As if the reality I'd built was tissue thin and I might tear through it with one Ill-timed stumble.

I came to a narrowing in the path and squeezed between two trees, only to realize that the tree to my right was the now-familiar yew tree with the carved initials. I was back in the clearing again. This time I didn't laugh. Something was happening here - either inside me or beyond my understanding. I couldn't decide which option was more terrifying. I backed away from the yew, into the center of the clearing and looked up into its spindly branches, which stretched into a seemingly impenetrable nest about twenty feet above my head.

Climb. The word seemed spoken aloud, but I knew its source was within my head. A young female voice, gently insistent. Should I? I used to love climbing trees and besides, I might be able to see out over the canopy and find my way out of this green and white labyrinth. As I took the first handhold, I realized that the birds had stopped singing. Huddled against the snow or holding their breath? Waiting to see if I would dare venture into their domain, perhaps.

My muscles were aching from the run, and the cumulative effect of the many months of manual labor and long, soul-cleansing runs. Nevertheless, I found the nub of a cut branch low enough to get my leg over and pulled myself up with both hands until I flopped over the lowest limb. I was an ungainly climber, very different from the monkey-like child I'd once been. Each tentative step onto a higher branch now came with an inner admonishment - this is dangerous.

Quickly though, I was high enough to grab

hold of the lower branches of the tangled nest that crowned the tree. I must have been about fifteen feet from the ground, but it felt like a hundred. I stretched a foot out but couldn't quite make the necessary next step. I'd have to jump. This was stupid. I should climb down. If I fell, I'd surely break something, and nobody would find me until morning.

I leapt, slipped and slapped my knee against the trunk, grabbing serpentine branches to arrest my fall. Pain flared under the patella. I would pay for this misadventure. My misstep only made me more determined and I stretched up with both hands and pulled myself into the heart of the tree.

Unfortunately, I was several feet yet from being able to see out over the treetops. I stopped to catch my breath and watch it billow out before me. For a second, it almost seemed to take the shape of a face, a female one, then it dissipated. A trick of the light, or of the dark, for certain.

Three or four minutes later, I had shinned up the next stout section of trunk, and was holding on for dear life, as the tree gently shook to and fro over the forest canopy. I stepped out onto a limb, braced myself, and looked.

I was right in the middle of the forest but I could see the road beyond the southern perimeter, and a thin blue-grey line of sea beyond the distant cliffs, although the whole scene was blurred by the incessant snow, tumbling down from a white sky that was turning a little pink along the horizon. It must be close to 4pm and nightfall wasn't far off.

Encouraged that I now knew where I was going, I was about to begin the challenging descent when I froze. I'd felt a tiny puff of warmth at the back of my neck. Wet warmth. Something unmistakable - breath.

I span round, but nothing was there. I listened. There was a slight gasp, as of indrawn air. Was someone holding his or her breath - someone other than me? Of course, I was alone in the tree, my imagination running rife against the background hum of nameless fear, the primal, animal sense of foreboding we sometimes feel in wild, natural places.

I began stiffly to climb down, being especially careful to have three solid foot- or handholds, before choosing the fourth. I made it back down to the nest of branches and was squinting down through the boughs, choosing a safe route down, when something moved below, something pale and oval - a face, with straw-blonde hair half-hidden under a lacy bonnet and eyes stark, wide and terrifyingly green. Skin almost translucently white, like the snow. A sorrowful stare, moving behind a trellis of branches and then slipping away into darkness.

I panicked, knowing instinctively that the person watching me was not quite of this world. My left foot slid off a limb caked with snow and green moss and I thudded down onto an unyielding bough, grasping blindly for a branch. The one I grabbed broke entirely away from the nest, through which I inevitably tumbled, crashing to the ground on my upper back and shoulders and rolling onto my side. A spike of pain and a cold stab of fear suffused me. I opened my eyes, curled in a fetal position among the roots of the yew and found I was still grasping the broken branch.

But when I looked at it, planning to use it as a crutch to lift myself to my feet, I discovered it wasn't a branch. It was a bone - probably a shinbone - grey-green with lichen and the dirt of ages. It was then that I must have passed out, the last sound I heard a ripple of girlish laughter.

"Ah, he's coming to now, poor lad."
A kindly voice insinuated itself into my consciousness and I opened my eyes to find a stout, concerned woman in her sixties dabbing my brow with a warm cloth, soaked in something stringently herbal. I started instinctively.

"Don't worry dear, you're amongst friends now," my nurse said.

I turned my head, saw a sideways confusion that resolved into a cozy cottage interior - a slightly chintzy attic bedroom, with a sloped ceiling on one side. A familiar, stick-thin figure tottered into the room from the top of a staircase carrying a tray loaded with tea things. The village postman - Keith - out of uniform but instantly recognizable from his gait. He winked, his angular, weathered face mischievous.

"I told you running in all weathers wasn't good for you," he admonished, setting down the tray. "This is Margery, my wife."

I sat up a little against plump cushions and attempted a smile of gratitude, although I was both bewildered and in an alarming amount of pain.

"Here, take these," Margery said, popping two pills into my mouth and letting me wash them down with a sip of water from a glass she held out. "Painkillers - got them for my back. They work wonders."

I didn't bother to work through the sense, or lack of it, of swallowing the mystery medication - I was in too much agony not to comply. And wonderfully, within twenty minutes, the pain did lift, and I was able to sit up against the pillows

Over a cup of tea (I am something of a caffeine addict, so this intervention was much appreciated) Keith explained how I'd come to end up in his spare bedroom. He'd been cycling back from his rounds, eager to get back to the warmth of home, when he'd seen something unusual - what looked like a body slumped against a hawthorn hedge on the fringes of the forest.

I stopped him there. "Did you say on the edge of the forest?"

"That's right," he explained. "Where the burn vanishes into the culvert. "Just off the road."

"And how was I lying?" I asked. Keith frowned as if this was rather beside the point.

"You were sort of sitting up, in that bit that overhangs. Were you trying to get out of the snow?"

I shook my head, baffled. I'd fainted under the tree, hadn't I?

"Anyways," Keith continued. "I thought you were a goner. You were still breathing but shivering all over and not responding to me at all. I called Marge and she drove down, and we got you back up here in the car. Doc's on the way but he's coming from Margate - only the coastal road's open. It's fair coming down out there."

Margery then elaborated on my recovery, an improvised process involving an electric blanket, hot water bottles and a balaclava. Apparently, I'd been delirious for a couple of hours before finally falling into a comfortable sleep. It was now 9pm and I gratefully accepted the Cloughs' offer to stay the night. After a hot bath that finally thawed the last remnants of the cold from my bones, I sat down to dinner with Keith and Margery. As his wife ladled hot stew onto my plate, Keith suddenly bolted, long-limbed, from the room. He returned holding something silvery.

"I nearly forgot... you were clutching this in your hand. I could barely get your fingers off of it."

He dangled a piece of jewelry at me - a silver locket, antique, on a thin chain. I took it, quite sure I'd seen it before but uncertain where. On its front, the locket had an unusual design - a snake coiled in a circle, eating its tail.

"Ouroboros", Margery said, surprising only me.

Keith nodded proudly. "She does the crossword every day. Is she a relative of yours?"

Keith was indicating the locket. I pressed the tiny catch on its side and opened it up. Inside, blurry but defiant, was a photograph - the face of a young girl, fair-haired and pale, with a penetrating gaze.

"I don't know her," I lied.

It was several days until I felt well enough, and the roads were clear enough, for me to venture into town. Keith drove me home the afternoon after my accident. The barn, although watertight, now proved itself to be far from airtight, as icy winds howled through the boards of the angled ceiling. I had the same dream for three nights in a row - I'm running in the wood and a girl (or perhaps two girls) are running after me and laughing. When I turn around, I see nobody, only my own footsteps fading away into nothingness. Sometimes it felt more like a memory than a dream.

My head was ablaze with questions and I was

almost feverish with the need to know more about the wood and its uncanny inhabitant. More prosaically, I knew I had to report the mysterious shinbone to the local police. I had two house calls to make.

Walking into town to exercise my aching limbs, I wandered into Remington's Antique's House, a cornucopia of ancient tat whose window I'd examined several times since I moved to the village, although I'd never been in. A bell rang above the door as I entered a musty, dusty storehouse of forgotten things.

An ornate dresser was heaped with mother of pearl inlaid jewelry boxes. A chaise longue was the resting place for a pyramid of greying books. A stack of old tennis racquets leaned against an ornate Japanese screen. In pride of place was a fully rampant stuffed bear, wearing a ladies' hat, wide-brimmed and decorated with purple paper roses.

One the far side of the room, lit by a shaft of tobacco-stained sunlight, was a glass counter under which sparkled a dragon's horde of bangles, necklaces, tiaras and cufflinks. Behind this was the round, jovial face of a woman I'd passed in the street several times and smiled back at.

"You'll be the new tenant at Forgehead Farm," she said, extending a ruddy hand.

"Owner actually," I said. "For my sins. I'm sorry, I don't know…"

"Jill Remington, daughter of the famous Bill," she replied.

I assumed I was supposed to know who the famous Bill was but didn't ask for clarification.

"I've been meaning to come in for ages," I lied. "I found something in the wood, and I wondered if you might be able to shed some light on it."

I felt a flicker of hesitation about handing the locket over, then a suggestion of breath on my neck (but it was merely a two-bar heater with a fan, stationed nearby on a pile of old magazines).

Jill studied the locket, pushing a pair of reading glasses further up her nose. She didn't speak for almost a minute and I began to wonder if something was wrong. I was about to clear my throat, but abruptly, Jill straightened and announced:

"You're in luck. As well as running this place, I'm the chairperson of the village historical society, and I know exactly who that is. Her name is Elizabeth Bailey."

Jill then proceeded to tell me an extraordinary story. Elizabeth has been the youngest daughter of the Hedgecombe family, who had owned Forgehead Estate. The one-hundred-acre estate had once included the farmhouse whose haybarn I was currently renovating. The manor on the Northern side of the hill, beyond the forest, was in fact still under the ownership of a branch of the venerable Hedgecombe dynasty. Their lineage went back at least four centuries.

Elizabeth had lived in the manor with her two older brothers, mother, father and several enormous deerhounds.

The Hedgecombe daughter was born around 1895, Jill thought, although some of the parish birth records appeared to be incomplete in that period. What could be gleaned from the meticulously maintained household ledgers is that, as well as the usual transient servants and old retainers, the family obtained the services of a French au pair and live-in tutor around the turn of the century, Madame Bouvier. The Madame brought with her from Epernay, her own daughter Elodie, just two years Elizabeth's junior. The innovative notion was that the girls would be co-educated by Madame Bouvier and learn one another's languages and cultures.

The two became fast friends, and in their teens scarcely separable. So much so that when they were finally separated, following Madame Bouvier's dismissal for instilling unwholesome morals in the girls, and an unnamed outrage the local newspapers would not elaborate upon, both girls wept for days.

Two weeks later, as Madame Bouvier packed her things in a local guesthouse, with the plan of returning home to France, her daughter Elodie vanished. She was never seen again, without even a letter to explain her whereabouts or any witnesses to shed light on the disappearance. The village feared the worst and to their credit, the Hedgecombes paid for a thorough search involving the police, coastguard and every able-bodied man and woman in the locality. It was to no avail.

"And what happened to Elizabeth?" I asked.

Jill sighed, as if delivering recent bad news.

"I'm afraid she went quite mad, had to be committed and caught the Spanish flu from a fellow inmate. She died the day before her sixteenth birthday."

I shivered, despite the heater liberally roasting my rear nearby. I looked at my watch, hastily thanked Jill for her information and headed uphill to the little local police station.

The following morning a cherry-picker was arranged, and a screen assembled around the yew tree. I was allowed inside to direct the forensic team and the arborealist they had called upon to oversee the removal of Elodie Bouvier's remains from the tree. Photos were taken of the position of the bones, which I found surprising - were the police really going to investigate a century old tragedy?

31

Also at hand was a well-dressed and shivering aristocratic man in his fifties. He introduced himself as Alasdair Hedgecombe, and he was the great, great grandson of Elizabeth's elder brother Michael.

"I felt it fitting to draw a line under this… smear upon our family. I believe my ancestors did this poor girl a grave disservice."

I wasn't exactly sure what he meant until the forensic team carried the bones down from the yew and laid them upon a tarpaulin. They had also found an empty bottle of a popular opiate, once used to alleviate gout, and quite lethal if drunk in a large enough dose.

To think a vibrant soul now amounted to little more than this collection of forgotten fragments seemed deeply sad. What made the tears come, however, were the words Elodie had written in her faltering English on the scrap of miraculously preserved paper in her pinafore pocket.

My heart lies here because my love will not. Elizabeth you were my beloved and if they don't accept, is the world's loss. I will always be your Cherie.

I remembered a detail Jill had told me about the ouroboros design on the locket, now clearly a love token.

"The Victorians we're obsessed with symbols," she had said, "and you need to be careful how you decode them. Nowadays we see the snake eating its tail as an emblem of futility, of something sinister, of doom even. At the turn of the century it meant unending love, the circle of life, an eternal pledge."

I didn't give the locket to Jill, or to the police. I wear it around my neck whenever I run in the Weirwynd Wood, as I am no longer afraid to do. I wear it to remind me that some loves never end, even though mine did. I wear it to remember Elodie and Elizabeth, to grant them the forgiveness they were never allotted in life.

No living relative locatable, the remains of Elodie Bouvier were interred in the Hedgecombe family plot, within sight of the house and the woods they loved to explore together. Elizabeth's grave was within touching distance of Elodie's. The burial was a fitting and graceful ceremony, attended by a handful of villagers, including Keith, Margery and Jill and presided over by Michael Hedgecombe, who I noted was accompanied by his husband Louie. I now realized why the tragic suicide of his ancestors' amour fou meant so much to him. I wasn't entirely clear why it meant so much to me.

Except, delirium and hallucinations notwithstanding, I somehow believed I knew Elizabeth and Elodie. I had looked into the deep green eyes of one, felt the other's breath. Elodie had entrusted me with her keepsake and I believed Elizabeth had saved my life by bringing me, somehow, to the edge of the wood.

As I watched a light smirr drift over the graves of the two girls, I knew that, touching as the ceremony had been, the thwarted lovers didn't really lie here, in the family graveyard. Well, not the part of them that mattered. Their souls were surely still laughing, chasing one another forever round the maze of little lanes around Weirwynd Wood.

I ran with them, and with my own ghosts, and we were at peace.

The Mississauga Ghoul

Flynn pushed a button on his watch and the dial glowed pale green. Four thirty-five. One more circuit and he'd be done. Tomorrow he had three and a half hours' drive to Detroit, with maybe a lunch stop in Lansing and he'd be ready for the big fight. Well, not the "big" fight. That had been last year. The battle of all battles that had launched Flynn Miller into the big time – Great Lakes Heavyweight Champion 2018. At the age of thirty-two, pushing it for a semi-pro, Flynn has sent an almighty haymaker from out of nowhere, launching that pituitary case Jackson "the ghoul" Bradley onto the canvas for a third-round count of ten.

Okay, there had been a knuckle-duster secreted in the glove, hastily removed and concealed by his corner boy, but Flynn has been due the win, after all the jeering and baying of Jackson's home crowd, calling Flynn a redneck trailer trash nobody and an old boy.

Sure, the black giant from Mississauga had it coming.

Flynn pushed on through the diagonal assault of rain becoming sleet becoming snow, skirting the edge of the Hardy Dam Pond. As his feet crunching iced-over snow, he swung his fists left and right close to his face, then wide in a series of one-two attacks, all the while feeling the chill seeping through his leggings. He'd turn off the trail at the Dam and run as fast as he could along that sometimes dangerous strip of highway back to his brother's shack, where he'd spent the last week mentally preparing himself to defend his title.

There would be big money in it for Flynn if he won again. One hundred thousand dollars. Not life-changing money for some, perhaps, but enough to pay off his brother's loan shark and a chunk of his own mortgage. Maybe enough to impress Jenny enough to give their marriage another go? Definitely enough to buy a new bicycle for Ellie-May. There was no knowing where a windfall like that might carry him.

The snow was brutal, chilling his face despite the muffler and beanie he'd pulled down hard over his ears. He felt his size thirteens slipping on the wet leaves beneath the snow and wished he'd taken up his brother's offer of trail shoes. Maybe if he went out again tomorrow morning…

Wait a minute… had he just missed the turning for the road? Flynn should have seen headlights through the gloom by now. Another half hour and it'd be pitch black and of course, he'd also refused a head torch. Flynn wasn't used to proper darkness. You never really got that in Detroit, where the skyscrapers and streetlights cut the skyline into shimmering facets.

No, this wasn't right. Flynn had trotted into a small clearing, where the remains of an old boat rotted away like the breastbone of a beached whale. The water must flood this high sometimes, Flynn thought, struggling and failing to get a useful signal on his phone. He'd not passed that boat on his last pass, but he couldn't have gone far astray. He could turn back and retrace his footsteps; but Flynn hated turning back.

Whump! A soft impact hit between his shoulder blades. A confused bird? No… a circular hole in the new-fallen snow contained a hard, round snowball, still intact. Thud! Another one bounced off his shoulder, stinging.

"What the fuck?"

The third snowball, more of an iceball, came from a totally different direction, hitting him full in the forehead and sending him staggering back. When he shook his head free of shattered ice and put a hand there, he came away with a smear of blood.

"Right you assholes, where are you?"

Kids, most likely. Locals, who gathered at the boat to drink hooch, smoke meth and ambush strangers with stone-filled snowballs. And yet… was that a laugh? An adult laugh? The deep, basso rumble was probably just cars heading over the dam.

Shit! Flynn managed to duck in time as another snowball, heavily compacted and filled with gravel, shattered on the trunk of a nearby ponderosa. That had come from an altogether different direction. How many kids were there?

It wasn't in him to run away. Flynn was the Great Lakes Heavyweight Champion 2018, after all. Six foot four and two hundred and six pounds of hard-earned muscle and sinew wasn't going to run from a bunch of kids throwing snowballs, no matter how loaded the missiles were, or how well-directed.

"Hope you know who you're messing with, boys. Come out and show your faces!"

Flynn compacted a snowball between his meaty fists, adding gloves to the list of things he regretted not borrowing. The icy snow chilled his fingers and added an ache to the gnawing fear he was beginning to feel. He was just about to heft the snowball in some arbitrary direction when a missile caught him in the back of the head, sending him staggering. His foot caught a tree root and he sprawled over the carcass of the disused skiff.

Before he could rise, another snowball smashed into his jaw and Flynn felt something crack there, a sliver of raw pain shooting up into his skull. He tried to cry out, but sound didn't come. A sixth ball of ice smacked into his larynx, rendering attempts to scream impossible as Flynn staggered to his feet and spun around, frantically searching for his attackers.

There was nothing but a moving smear of shadow behind the trees on the far side of the clearing. A hazy shape there lacked form but looked nothing like a child. Too bulky, too weighty. A snowball hurtled out of the gloom, catching a shard of headlight. The road must be close! The snowball seemed to slow down as Flynn tried to spin round to evade it.

He ducked, and the snowball mirrored his move, impossibly swerving and looking like nothing so much as a gloved fist as it barrelled into his nose and eyes, blinding him, and breaking his septum.

Flynn felt himself whimpering now as he half staggered, half crawled out of the clearing the way he'd come, following his own footsteps, filling them with blood as the echo of a deep Canadian laugh rolled between the trees. The shape of a large man formed before him out of the absence of snow, an invisible presence revealed. A hooded figure, poised and ready for the next swing. The Mississauga Ghoul had come to claim his stolen title.

It wasn't fair. How could Flynn have known the knockout would cause a delayed haemorrhage? The Ghoul had died eighteen hours after the fight. There had been plenty of time for his manager, his trainer, his wife… or someone to have seen the symptoms and rushed him to the ER. Okay, Flynn had cheated but that massive ape had provoked him.

The last snowball found him as Flynn got back onto his feet on the trail on top of the embankment. It came floating across the water, impossibly, inescapably driving his left eye deep into its socket and pulverizing Flynn's skull as he slipped and toppled through the thin icy veneer of the freezing reservoir. An invisible crowd roared.

As the Great Lakes Heavyweight Champion sank into the pristine water, beams from the headlights and taillights of passing cars pulsed over the shattered ice above him. Red for the glove that killed him, white for the canvas that embraced his final fall.

Overleaf

I'd always wanted to own and run a bookshop and finally, at the age of fifty-five, I'm doing just that. It might have cost me my marriage, my health (two heart attacks within five years) and my nerves (I'm on daily anti-anxiety medication) but Overleaf Books is finally a reality. If you take the correct turning off Edinburgh's Royal Mile and negotiate the somewhat erratic steps on Carrubber's Close, you'll find us.

The stone arches of my shop used to contain the wine cellars of a now-defunct inn, as well as the stables for travellers' horses. Now they are filled with the wit, wisdom, and waywardness of thinkers and entertainers from across the globe, stretching from a new translation of Beowulf to critiques of post-modernism. I shamelessly curate my collection, rather than simply filling my limited floorspace with Harry Potter ephemera. When I decided to realise my dream, I was perfectly aware that the publishing industry, particularly in terms of traditional books, was in decline. It didn't bother me. At the very least, the lack of customers allows me to indulge my love of reading and perhaps I'll finally finish that historical novel I've been writing about the Highland Clearances. I sell just enough books to keep the shop afloat and I'm thinking of coming off the Sertraline. Living the dream, some might say.

Recently, however, something decidedly odd has been happening. I took on a part-time assistant four weeks ago, more to allow me to take the occasional break or go to the bathroom, as for any economic reason. Her name is Emily and she's a philosophy student who, fortunately, shares my high degree of tolerance for silence and solitude. She's also something of an alphabetical savant, able to shelve a trolley-load of books in a matter of minutes. Finally, Emily possesses multiple facial piercings and a hard stare that would make Paddington quail. She is not prone to superstitious imaginings, nor does she seem the type for elaborate pranks, so when she came to me on a wet Tuesday morning, just before closing, with an ashen face, I was immediately concerned.

"What is it, Emily?" I enquired.

"John," she began, almost embarrassed, "someone keeps turning the books round."

She led me down to the lower arches, which are accessed from the main room by a small flight of wooden steps. You have to duck as you descend, a precaution I'd failed to take all too often. If Emily hadn't been with me, I might have suspected that one of my regular head injuries was responsible for what I saw. On every shelf lining the small arched space, occasional books had been turned round, so that their spines faced inward, and the pale edge of their pages stood out between the spines of the more conventionally arrayed titles. All in all, there must be fifty or more books misfiled in this way.

I turned to my young colleague with an unfinished question on my lips. "Emily, who could have…?"

"Well, nobody," she said hastily, "I was down here just five minutes ago, and the shelves were fine. We've not had any customers since then."

She let the implication hang, as we both set about turning the books back around and tried to dispel any spooky assumptions.

"I… I guess I might have missed someone," said Emily without any real conviction in her voice. "A customer could have slipped past me." She didn't sound very convinced.

I replaced the last book, a Tenniel-illustrated "Alice in Wonderland", and we shut up the shop without a further word on the subject, emerging onto the Royal Mile as a delicate rose-hued sunset began.

The following morning, I was due to open up by myself, Emily having a full programme of lectures on Wednesday mornings. I switched everything on, prepared the float for the till and read through the morning's emails and online orders (yes, I'll admit, I bowed to my nephew's suggestion to join the 21st century and now sell roughly 40% of my books via the internet). All that time I was resisting an urge to run downstairs and check the shelves, almost a fear that I'd see something I could not explain. By the time I finally gave in to this urge, just three minutes before opening time, I had prepared myself for a world-shattering revelation. I crept down the stairs and turned the corner like a M .R. James-styled academic tiptoeing into a crypt.

Fortunately, nothing had evidently changed overnight, and the books were arrayed just as perfectly and rationally as ever. Relieved, I exhaled a deep breath I hadn't even realised I'd been holding and went to unlock the front doors. Forty minutes later, I had my first customer, a jovial middle-aged woman who bought three books, including a Complete Borges story collection, which to my mind, marked her as a reader of rare distinction.

"I do like your unconventional filing system," she said, as she presented her card for payment.

"My what?" I asked, reaching for the complementary bookmarks.

"Turning every thirteenth book to the wall. It really piques curiosity!"

I smiled grimly and handed her a tote bag of her purchases then, the minute she left the shop, dashed downstairs to the cellar to investigate. As my customer had intimated, the strange phenomenon had happened again. I counted the books between those turned around. There were indeed twelve with their spines out for every reversed text.

My mind began to race. My friend Jamil has a spare set of keys for the shop, in case of emergencies and because he lives within a twenty-minute walk of the old town, but he's a barrister without any evident sense of humour or love of practical jokes. It couldn't be him, surely.

Next, I looked at the specific books which had been turned around, to see if there was any linking theme, any clue as to why these individual books should be manhandled in this way.

Edwin Abbott's Flatland, Tolkien's The Silmarillion, Kingsley's Water Babies, a popular science book about the Many Worlds interpretation of quantum physics, Aristophanes' The Birds, the Complete Novels of Franz Kafka. The phantom book-turner perhaps had a penchant for fantasy, but I could see little else to link the titles and, besides, I too enjoy books about alternative realities; such subject matter is to be found everywhere on Overleaf's shelves.

As I turned the errant books round, I decided that at lunchtime I'd call Jamil and Emily to check whether either of them had perhaps inadvertently loaned the shop keys to a trickster acquaintance. That had to be the explanation. When I had almost completed my repair job, I could hear someone clearing their throat in the main room – evidently, I'd missed the sound of the little Victorian bell by the door that tinkles whenever someone enters the shop.

I went upstairs to help Mr Andropolous, a regular customer, who was buying a present for his granddaughter and trying to decide which of the two pocket birdwatching guides was best. Advising him took no more than five minutes. I managed to persuade Mr Andropolous to get both titles (I am not entirely without sales nous). Then, without any conscious thought leading my footsteps that way, I found myself descending to the cellar once more. What I saw there came close to giving me my third heart attack.

At least seventy books had magically inverted themselves, this time taking as their organising principle the Fibonacci sequence. Two reversed books, then a gap of two, then another back to front title, and then gaps of three, five, eight, thirteen, twenty-one and so forth. It staggered me.

"Who's here?" I found myself asking the walls, an audible quaver in my voice. This was crazy. Someone must have sneaked by me, while I'd been intent on discussing Scottish seabirds with Mr Andropolous.

There was no reply. I began removing books from the shelves, this time noticing that the titles seemed to have nothing at all in common. The book-moving wraith had evidently focused purely on its mathematical scheme this time round. I opened one of the books, the Everyman edition of Wuthering Heights, and turned to the last page, my eyes flicking down to the famous last lines. *...how anyone could ever* *imagine unquiet slumbers, for the sleepers in that quiet earth.* All well and good except now it was the penultimate line of the novel, which somehow now ended thus:

And yet, given the tumultuous passage of those lives, I fancied I might yet catch the sound of some anguished soul adrift on the wind; I listened then, and am listening still.

What? That's not how I remembered the book's conclusion. Was this some alternative manuscript, an academic oddity? I flicked to the frontispiece, but it presented no answers. I chose another reversed book, to see if it too had been tampered with. Primo Levi's The Periodic Table. This was a book I'd read and loved as a young man, but I was sure I couldn't quote anything from it. Nevertheless, I turned to the contents page and all seemed present and correct...21 chapters, each named after a different chemical element. There was a second copy of the book, this one spine-out, on the shelf beside the reversed text, so I compared their contents. Immediately I spotted a discrepancy. Instead of Levi's chapter on

Cerium, in the misfiled book there was one on Antimony, a rare metal used in bullets, batteries and bearings. The chapter was the same length as the Levi original but told a wholly different story.

Now I was more than baffled. I was worried. I ran upstairs and locked the front door, then returned to my enquiries. I made a pile of the reversed books and began to go through them. There was a copy of Ulysses whose final chapter ended with a capitalised and resounding *NO!* There was a slim Murakami volume, What I Talk About When I Talk about Swimming, and a series of crime novels by Patricia Highsmith-Jones. Even Dante's Inferno was radically different, consisting of four sections, the final one being Oblio, which detailed the eventual slowing down and diminution of the universe, a heat-death predicted 700 years before physicists posited the steady-state entropic annihilation of all that we know.

I was agog. There could be no ready explanation for this. I was either the victim of some infernally devious, conceptual prank or...

what exactly? I couldn't even begin to formulate a coherent explanation. Feeling suddenly weak at the knees, I grabbed for the nearest shelf, needing to feel something solid between my fingers. I was lost in a Borgesian labyrinth of equally untenable possibilities. I have no idea how long I stood there, propped up like a listing stack of books, numb with incomprehension. Eventually my concentration was shattered by a harsh knocking on the front door. I looked at my watch. 3.10pm. I had somehow lost two hours.

I ran to let Emily in – she'd been due to join me at 3pm and had been knocking and trying to call the shop landline for ten minutes. She looked concerned by my evidently distracted appearance, and I hastily explained what had transpired.

"Can you think of anyone who might possibly have obtained your keys?" I asked.

"Not at all," she replied demonstrating that her shop keys were on the same fob as her home set, which she kept on her person at all times.

"Then, it must be one of Jamil's friends. I must call him. But first... come and see," I insisted, leading Emily down to the lower floor. There, both of us came face to face with a paradigm-shifting vision and our worlds altered forever. The pile of books in the middle of the floor had vanished and every single book was back on the shelves, except with their spines facing towards the walls, along with every other title in the shop. Emily ran upstairs and witnessed the same phenomenon there too. Shelf after shelf of unknowably mysterious texts, the whiteness of all those edges actually making the room a little brighter, reflecting more of the fluorescent illumination. The transformation was complete, and it had taken approximately ninety seconds.

I no longer felt afraid. In fact, laughed aloud, which probably did little to reassure my concerned employee as to the status of my sanity. We picked a few books off the shelves and I was easily able to demonstrate that they were almost exactly, but not quite like the corresponding books in our own world.

"What do you mean our own world?" Emily asked, taken aback. "No way…"

"It's the only explanation. I didn't do this. Believe me!"

I could tell Emily wasn't sure what to believe, as we replaced the books, this time leaving the others as they were. I'd had a notion we might try an experiment. We turned a dozen texts around, spines facing out, as it should be. We both closed our eyes, entirely aware that what we were doing felt crazy.

"No cheating now," I insisted. "Eyes firmly shut and count to one hundred."

We both did so, aloud, giving the invisible book fairies adequate opportunity to work their magic. It was with a palpable sense of disappointment, therefore, when we opened our eyes to see that nothing had changed. The colourful spines of the few books we'd replaced stood out against long lines of undifferentiated white paper.

"I suppose you could claim it's a new concept in bookselling," Emily offered wryly. I laughed, despite my bafflement, a hollow laugh that

57

developed into a full, hysterical fit of giggles. It was a moment or two after the echoes of that laugh died away that I heard it.

A faint voice – my own voice – muffled and indistinct. The delicate hint of an Ayrshire accent, the slight lisp on Fs that is part of my idiolect. Undeniably me, but elsewhere. Actually, somewhere specific... the voice issuing from behind the stacks, murmuring in amazement the phrase:

"Emily...come see... it's happening again."

The Three Sisters

Hannah had a quandary, and a painfully pressing one at that. She was thirty-eight years old, and the fertility specialist had just informed her that her likelihood of conceiving a child was vanishingly slim and dwindling with every passing year. To make matters worse, she'd just discovered that the main reason her husband of nine years was no longer sleeping with her was not due to his diminished libido following a rugby injury, but rather that he'd been having an affair with a much younger work colleague. Mark didn't know that Hannah was aware of the affair, which had been going on for almost two years now. Not yet, at any case.

She'd had her suspicions for a while, and had confirmed them by following Mark to one of his "squash" games, to discover that the only games Mark was playing were with his marriage. Hannah, a lapsed Catholic, had assumed that this sort of textbook infidelity was beyond a man as prosaically bland as her quantity surveyor husband, whom she'd married largely for his reliability. How naïve she'd been. Now she released that the continuously delayed baby she'd been asking for would probably never come. Not unless she did something desperate.

A long, boozy lunch with her purple-haired school friend Natalie later, Hannah had devised a plan, one that anyone else she told, other than Natalie, would have deemed crazy. Of course, she didn't want to stay with Mark any longer than necessary. She simply needed his seed. She'd considered various means of extracting his genetic essence, but the procedure was too challenging and knowing her luck, Hannah would probably kill him in the process. Murder wasn't quite on her mind. Nor could she afford to visit a sperm bank – not on her salary. There had to be another way.

Blackmail was a possibility; persuading him to impregnate her in exchange for her silence regarding the affair. Embarrassing Mark with his family wouldn't work – they were fairly incorrigible atheists from Edinburgh -- investment brokers, ad executives and the like. But his colleagues, perhaps? Hannah had quickly discounted the idea. Mark was a vindictive type, and she didn't fancy the notion of having sex with someone who despised or feared her. Plus, she had the notion that any child conceived in resentment would never turn out well. No – Mark had to think he was just fulfilling his conjugal duty. Ideally, he'd get her with child and then she could divorce him at her leisure.

"It's going to sound nuts," Natalie had said, as Hannah was exploring her options out loud in the Peebles tea shop they frequented. "But I know a spell that might work, and a place to cast it."

Natalie, as well as owning the village's 'spiritual supplies' shop, full of rose quartz crystals and dream catchers, was a practicing Wiccan white witch. Hannah seldom delved deep into this inscrutable and frankly laughable aspect of her friend's life, but she was desperate now, and willing to give credence to anything. She'd almost certainly regret what she said next, but then needs must when you have an achingly empty nest.

"Go on then. Spill."

On Sunday morning, instead of going to her usual yoga class, Hannah drove out along the country lanes, to a quiet car park by an old stone bridge and stood gazing into the River Tweed, reciting Natalie's spell over and over in her head (it wouldn't do to say the words aloud, not yet). When she was ready, she forced the woolly hat down over her ears and put on the walking boots she'd stashed under the passenger seat footwell. On the seat beside her was her kit bag containing the rolled-up yoga mat, towel, and a change of clothes she'd never use. She gulped down some water from her reusable bottle – it wouldn't do for it still to be full when she returned, although this measure granted her husband a degree of acuity she was sure he lacked.

Hannah locked the car, crossed the bridge, walked a little way up the road and found the narrow footpath under coppery beech trees which led uphill towards the Three Brethren.

"I don't think of them as brothers," Natalie

had explained. "To me they're clearly sisters. I mean they're bloody egg-shaped, after all."

On the top of the hill sat three eight-foot-high cairns, constructed from crudely cut granite slabs somewhere around the sixteenth century and renovated across the intervening centuries. Nobody knew entirely what they meant, but a metal plaque positioned nearby offered the speculation that they marked the perimeter of lands once belonging to the Lairds of Yair.

"Liars of Yair, more like," Natalie had opined. "They're a witches' meeting place, more like. Clearly a perfect place to cast spells."

Hannah hadn't known how serious her friend was but if her ridiculous plan was to have any efficacy, then she had to take her spellcasting seriously. Location was paramount, and these ovoid monuments, atop a wind and rain-scoured hilltop, were perfect.

As Hannah picked her way up the rocky slopes leading to the top of the hill named after the Brethren, she began to regret not mixing in a little cardio with the yoga. She was quickly breathless, with two hundred feet still to climb. How had she never taken this walk before? Mark and Hannah had lived in Peebles for almost five years.

She paused her ascent to catch her breath and look around. The sky was overcast, full of glowering rainclouds. Drizzly mist obscured much of the valley. This was a shame – the Southern Upland Way ought to provide a spectacular view on a clear day. Perhaps this dreich murk was more appropriate, however, given what she had in mind.

Twenty minutes later, pushing her hands down on her thighs for added momentum, Hannah felt the rocky ground begin to level below her. The scrubby forest to her right fell away as the rounded top of the hill presented itself. Wind and slanting rain were now blasting the left side of her face into numbness. Stray red hairs fluttered out from under her hat to stick to her icy cheek, almost as if trying to hide the Malta-shaped ruddy red birthmark she had there, a blemish that Mark had once jokingly called her 'witch's mark'. He'd never have guessed that his teasing joke would become one day become prophecy.

At first, it looked like there was only one cairn marking the hilltop. Then, as Hannah climbed the last few feet, two more hove into view. Fortunately, nobody was about, and why on Earth would they be, a little before 8am on a viciously inclement September morning? The elements were whipping the stones, and Hannah, with violent turbulence – veils of mist and lashing rain stung her reddened cheeks.

Hannah walked into the centre of the stones. There were three verses in the short rhyme she'd learned. Each must be directed towards a unique stone, a different sister. Perhaps the stones were androgynous? Genderfluid, in modern parlance.

She stretched out a hand and touched the first stone. It felt surprisingly warm, but perhaps that was just because her fingers were so icy. Withdrawing her hand, she took out the craft knife she'd concealed in her jeans pocket, uncapping its lid. Could she really do this?

Taking a deep breath, Hannah drew the blade

sharply across the palm of her left hand. The knife cut deeper than she'd expected, blood instantly welling to the wound.

"Fucking hell", she said, forgetting herself and pressing her hand against her jeans. It left a bloody smear. Shit, Hannah thought, I'll have to change into my yoga leggings later. She looked at her hand. The wound was an inch long and bleeding profusely. Not so deep that a plaster wouldn't cover it, though. Not deep enough to need stitches. She had tissues in her other pocket but for now, she needed the blood to keep flowing.

Leaning towards the cold stone, Hannah pressed her hand firmly against the granite.

> *Stones of the earth, stones of the sky*
> *Bring me a wee bairn, by and by...*

The spell, adapted by Natalie, was nothing if not literal. Hannah spun on her heels and walked over to the second stone. Her hand throbbed. The wind blew at her back now, almost knocking her off her feet. This stone felt a little colder, since it bore the full brunt of the tumultuous weather.

Take from my hand the pulse of my blood
Take from my breath, and let it do good

She exhaled deeply, exactly as she'd been told, a cloud of breath blowing out over the surface of the stone. Was it really that cold up here? She moved to the third stone, noting with satisfaction the red stain her wound had left on the second.

Take from these words and take from this art
A life for a life, and a new beating heart.

Hannah swallowed fearfully, hearing herself complete the incantation. Some fragment of her Catholic upbringing quailed at the blasphemy of it.

The third stone anointed, Hannah closed her eyes and counted to ten, arms outstretched, rotating slowly, and trying not to fall over. When she was at the end of her count, she heard a voice.

"Oh, sorry, are we interrupting?"

She opened her eyes. Two hillwalkers; a father and son. Hannah would have blushed if her cheeks weren't already ruddy red. She closed her left hand to hide the wound, hoped the hikers hadn't seen the dark stains on the stones.

"Not at all, just being daft!" she explained with forced levity.

"No harm in that," smiled the father. "No harm at all."

Back at home, it seemed Hannah would get away with her subterfuge. Mark was out, having gone for a run. She knew this because his trail shoes were missing from the back door. Hannah scrubbed her jeans in the kitchen sink, getting most of the blood out, then threw them in the washing machine with a half load of other clothes. She washed her wound and put a big plaster on it. She'd say she cut it on a tin of fruit cocktail (her usual post-yoga treat).

Mark returned twenty minutes later, all sweaty and red-faced from his run. Not lying about his whereabouts for once, she thought. Then, remarkably, perhaps because she'd changed into the provocatively low V-necked red sweater and short denim skirt she knew he liked, and maybe also because he was flushed with post-run hormones, Mark grabbed her and pulled her into the shower with him. They hadn't had sex in the bathroom for almost a year, Hannah reckoned. Mark was rough but enthusiastic, and Hannah was happy to oblige. If this was the spell working its magic, so be it.

Later, while Mark watched his snooker semi-final in the spare room, Hannah called Natalie and told her everything. When she'd finished, Hannah was expecting an excited congratulations from her friend. Instead, Natalie said, following a moment's silence, "There's something I didn't tell you. If I had, you'd have not gone through with it."

Two days later, Natalie phoned in sick to her job as an administrator for a Leukaemia charity. Mark had already left for work, late as usual, speeding off in a shower of gravel in the Audi. She had the whole day to herself. Time to work up towards the terrible thing she had to do. It was obvious, in retrospect. It was there in the words of the incantation. A life for a life...

She took Tabitha, their tortoiseshell tabby, out into the garden shed, with the sharpest kitchen knife under her arm. Tabitha was placid, evidently having no sixth sense for her own imminent demise. Her eyes held the same comic disdain as ever, her slightly chubby body betraying no raised heartbeat as Hannah closed the door behind her and placed her pet on the dusty boards. Hannah sat on an upturned mop bucket and opened the can of tuna she'd brought, tossing a few chunks onto the floor with the point of the knife.

How could she do this? Hannah felt tears welling in her eyes at the very thought of it. She would surely go straight to hell, if such a place turned out to exist. A poor, innocent animal, albeit one with a tendency to scratch strangers. Tabitha was crouching to gobble down the delicious fish in brine. Hannah could just grab her and plunge the knife into her back – it would be over in moments. She felt her heart beating wildly, as she moved her knife grip from and underhand to an overhand position. A stabbing stance.

Bzzzzzz!

Hannah jumped, as the phone in her back

pocket vibrated loudly. She wouldn't answer. A call now would definitely derail her frankly evil scheme.

Who was she kidding? She wasn't going to kill the cat! Hannah was the kind of person who painstakingly caught bluebottles under pint glasses and shepherded them outside, to buzz another day. She couldn't possibly murder a poor, defenceless animal, and certainly not a beloved pet. In that moment, Hannah felt a peculiar and unique cocktail of shame, relief, and disappointment.

She instinctively knew that even if she could locate the hedgehog who lived under the holly bush, she'd not be able to kill it, either. Hannah also suspected a worm or spider would not tip the balance of Wiccan power in her favour. Not an equivalent sacrifice.

Hannah tipped the rest of the tuna on the floor and silently apologised to the blithely voracious tabby cat, as the animal gulped it down.

Hannah didn't return any of the calls that came

through from Natalie, her mother-in-law or from the unknown number that kept trying. Instead, she opened a bottle of pinot grigio and proceeded to get drunk. It was only when she heard the stout rap on her front door and looked at her phone to find she'd missed seventeen calls, that Hannah realised something was seriously wrong.

There were two young police persons at the door – one male, one female. The woman officer spoke.

"Mrs Hannah McMillan? Is your husband named Mark?"

Hannah nodded mutely, feeling her heartbeat accelerating wildly for the second time that day. She leaned against the door jamb, at first because she wanted to appear more sober than she was, but also because she knew what was coming.

"I'm afraid we have some bad news. There's been an accident."

A freak accident, as it happened. On his way to work, blasting along the quiet border roads, Mark had evidently swerved to avoid something, possibly a roe deer, common around these parts. The Audi had collided with a digger which had chosen that moment to reverse out of a field. Mark had been projected through the windscreen into the digger's bucket. He'd not worn his seatbelt and had almost certainly died in an instant, his skull shattered. The airbag had failed to fire, which the manufacturers swore was all but impossible.

There were no skid marks on the road because Mark hadn't been able to brake. Somehow a plastic drinking bottle had rolled under the middle pedal, meaning that when he'd tried to jam on the brakes, nothing had happened. Even had he braked, there was only a slim chance he'd have survived, the coroner explained at Mark's inquest, as if that held any consolation.

The drink bottle was Hannah's. She'd brought it with her to cement her yoga-based alibi on the day of her spellcasting. The bottle had always annoyed her by being just a little too wide to fit into the Audi's cupholders.

Three weeks' later, following the inquest, the cremation, and the memorial, once she had finished weeping and an endurable numbness had replaced the constant guilt and terror she'd experienced after Mark's death, Hannah began to feel unaccountably nauseous each morning. She visited her local pharmacy with a strange sensation of sad excitement fluttering in her chest. An anxiety of hope and fear. Back at home, sitting on the toilet, staring at two faint, but undeniable, little lines, Hannah immediately knew one thing with certainty.

She'd have to be exceptionally careful not to irritate her friend Natalie from now on.

The Sanctified Shard

As the train clattered slowly towards the station at Tonbury, a cloud of steam from the engine three carriages ahead dissipated to reveal a frosty idyll. This December was like no other I'd experienced: crisp, shimmeringly bright and imbued with an air of expectant promise. I'd just turned twenty-four and had been tasked with my first solo project, attempting to accurately date the rose window at Tonbury Cathedral. I would be using a combination of microscopy, forensic investigation, and a thorough combing of the cathedral records.

Professor Angus Cruikshank of the University of Edinburgh had recently opined that the nine leaves making up the unique rose at the front of the chancel might pre-date the Norman conquest. My PhD supervisor, Dr Henry Wadham, thought this highly unlikely and felt it important that I investigate the provenance of the panes prior to the publication of my study of late Middle Ages cathedral design. I'd already had a hankering to add Tonbury to the list of Cathedrals I'd personally toured so I eagerly got in touch with the archbishop to arrange a visit. If I could complete my examination by the end of 1890, I might be able to publish by the following autumn, following the usual round of peer review and assessment. This, at least, was my scheme.

The cathedral appeared beyond the meadows, which were filled with an almost ethereal bed of low-lying mist. Its towers dominated the landscape and inspired just as much awe in our Victorian era as it must have done as our ancestors ended their pilgrimages here.

Tonbury itself proved to be a pleasingly quaint town, not much larger than Ely, which I'd visited in the autumn. Its cobbled lanes and crookedly leaning Tudor buildings made me half expect a hunting party led by the inestimable Henry to ride into courtyard of the little Inn in which I would be staying during my week-long enquiries. Fortunately, no such boisterousness disturbed my first evening in the Willow Inn, which was spent reading and playing draughts with Mr Eddington, a naturalist come to study rare varieties of toad in the marshes.

The following morning, with several hours to spare before my 11am meeting with the archbishop, I popped into the local telegraph office to send a message home to my fiancée Millie: REACHED TONBURY. CATHEDRAL IMPRESSIVE. ROOMS COMFORTABLE. SEEING ARCH THIS AM. LOVE, P.

The P stood for Peter, my Christian name, and I hoped the almighty would forgive me abbreviating his Tonbury representative. With my meagre academic stipend and a charge of a ha'penny a letter, it seemed a reasonable accommodation.

Task complete, I then went for a stroll cross the meadows, following a bridle path suggested to me by Mr Eddington, who'd discovered it just the other day. Beginning with a narrow lane lined with flinty walls, the path opened out into a dusty strip buttressed by hawthorn hedges, which snaked up a gentle hillside.

Gentle at first, I should say, for after twenty minutes of marching and finding myself frustrated in my desire for a view by the tall hedges on either side, the way began to incline exponentially, and narrow, leading me into a dense wood of spindly birches and alders. Even on this winter morning, with the sun low and occluded by thin clouds, I was soon sweating in my tweed three piece and overcoat. I took off my gloves and scarf and stuffed them into the haversack in which I kept my instruments and notebook.

Under the trees it was mercifully cooler, and I stomped up a rocky trail whose mud was fortunately frozen solid, offering purchase for my decidedly inappropriate brogues. I made a mental note to buy some decent boots in town. A few minutes later, my fervent wish for a vista was granted as the path levelled then burst from the trees onto a sloping meadow of astonishing beauty.

A gleaming river wormed its way across the valley floor, between rutted fields of ploughed earth and intermittent rectangles of corn stubble and still green grass. The sun shone between distant trees, illuminating patches of frost which glittered like diamond dust. Gnarled trees punctuated the scene, grasping at the pale sky. A murder of crows chattered darkly as they hopped among the corn stalks. To my right, the cathedral's tower asserted itself upon the horizon.

How remarkable that I'd be employed there in a matter of hours, making discoveries of potentially historic import! I felt a sudden pang that my beloved Millie couldn't be with me to revel in such a scene. Millicent, a schoolteacher, was very much with child, our first, and unable to travel due to her frequent bouts of nausea.

The fields to my left, below which the river wound, were bordered by a wooden fence which had seen better days. A line of crows perched upon it, eyeing me with suspicion. A moment of daft inspiration made me doff my homburg to them; I looked around for witnesses to my silliness. Fortunately, there were none.

My glance alighted upon an angled stone in the middle of a distant field, the bottom of which was lost in still-lingering morning mist. I'd heard there were palaeolithic standing stones in the vicinity – a half-crumbed circle and a series of lone menhirs – could this be one of them?

As there were no other pedestrians, and because I couldn't really see the harm of it, I clambered over a partially collapsed section of fence and tiptoed into the frost-hardened field, picking my way between the muddy striations. I was only a little disappointed when, a few hundred yards later I stood face to face with a simple, albeit elongated headstone, too decrepit to bear more than a trace of lettering. Not prehistoric, but possibly medieval in origin – could it be a mile-marker, for some long-forgotten footway?

"Thar's the grave of the Master o' Tonbury!" a voice cried out. I started.

A fellow had appeared upon a pony on the lane above me. I squinted against the sunlight to make him out.

"I'm s... sorry, I just wanted to take a look."

I headed back up towards the bridle path, and the stranger was quickly revealed to be a rustic type, possibly a farmer, chewing on a cornstalk as if he'd wandered into the scene from a Constable painting.

"No 'arm in lookin'" He opined. "Just so long as you 'int no relative."

"Relative?" I inquired, trying to clamber back over the fence with my dignity and gentleman's quarters intact.

"The Master, Duke o' Tonbury as was, used to have 'is mansion here, down by the water."

"Oh really?" I asked, more intrigued than embarrassed now.

"Yes. That were in sixteen oatcake, mind. I'm not handy with the specifics, but 'im 'ad 'is 'ouse burnt down by the locals, some say."

"Why on earth would they do that?"

"Said he was damnéd, or summat. He 'ad a 'art attack and died in his study, so I hears. They buried him under that stone, wrote only his first name – John – and left him to 'is ladies' mercy."

"His what?" I was genuinely perplexed by this sinister tale, particularly as the teller appeared to grow increasingly self-conscious as he related it, looking around him as if the crows might gossip about his loose tongue.

"'Ave said too much, as usual. And 'm late for county fair. Ben Maddox, at yer service."

He took off the cloth cap and gave a stiff little bow, while his nag squinted at me with undisguised loathing, snorting foul-smelling clouds of equine breath in my direction.

"Peter Pritchard, at yours," I remarked, as he rode unsteadily off. I watched the farmer recede over the brow of the hill then turned to look back into the meadow.

Beyond the stone, a small patch of mist seemed to cling to a bend in the river. Protruding from this reticent cloud were the fingers of a particularly damaged tree, which leaned over the unseen water, as if in supplication. It was the only tree in the vicinity and from where I stood, I couldn't tell whether it was naked from wintering, or from death.

A moment of panic seized me. I looked at my pocket watch. 10:25am. I was going to be late for the archbishop if I didn't continue apace. That wouldn't do at all.

"Here is our remarkable rose," said Archbishop Edwin Muncie with a grandiloquent gesture. I followed his hand up to the brightly illuminated circle of leaf-shaped panes, each decorated with complex leaded patterns in many colours, depicting the martyrdom of saints and the trials and teachings of the Christ. The window was fully forty feet in diameter and situated at least eighty feet above the flagstones. Fortunately, the trapezoid chancel was lined with a raised wooden gallery which afforded cathedral workers the opportunity to inspect and clean the glass.

The archbishop, despite his seventy-plus years, lifted the hem of his robe and nimbly climbed the spiral stair leading to this walkway, as I cautiously followed. The morning service had ended sometime prior, and the cathedral was empty save a few tourists and a pastor collecting discarded hymnals. Our voices echoed magnificently from the limestone surfaces.

"I'm so looking forward to finding out more about our glass. I believe it's a source of some controversy," the archbishop said, stepping back to let me pass and inspect the glowing circle that towered above me.

"There are competing theories," I replied, giving my most politic response. "I'll know more once I inspect it closely."

I stood on tiptoes and was barely able to get my eyes near to the surface of the lowest pane, which depicted Mary Magdalene washing the feet of Jesus. The pale blue glass depicting Mary's robes was laid in a series of triangular slices, beautifully capturing the falling folds of cloth.

"We have ladders, and even a wheeled scaffold," offered the archbishop, "although you'll want to inspect the latter closely before you commit. It's not been used in an age."

I thanked the prelate, whose face in that moment was lit in a beatific glow of late morning sunlight, coloured in pink and gold. Muncie led me to a concealed closet, where a stout set of tall stepladders were stationed. I have no great fear of heights, but their modern build reassured me, nonetheless. With these I'd be able to reach the centre of the pane, at the very least. Muncie kindly offered me a young chorister, Anthony, to assist, and we stationed the ladders beneath the rose and laid out my equipment upon a fold-out trestle table nearby.

Anthony, it transpired, was shy to the extent of being near-mute, which suited me fine. I'm not one for loquacity while I'm working. Instead of needlessly prattling, my attentive assistant passed me tools and instruments like a nurse attending an operation. Indeed, this was a delicate procedure, since this window rose was quite precious, whatever its provenance. Some of the panes had come a little loose from their leading, which allowed me to insert a small scraping tool between frame and pane and extract tiny fragments of glass which I might examine under my microscope later.

With an ordinary magnifying glass, it was already evident that some of this glass was much older than the bulk of the panes which, I estimated, dated from the fourteenth century. From the nature of the dyeing, the smoothness of the glass and the presence of evident layering and air bubbles I was able to identify several leaves dating much further back, potentially to the mid-eleventh century. The process was engrossing but intricate and time consuming. I took copious notes, having sketched the window first, so that I could annotate each pane with its putative date.

I was so captivated by my task that I hardly noted Anthony excusing himself and leaving, or the weather beyond the window changing. From a clear, crisp winter's day, the afternoon progressed into a darkening storm, whose rain blattered against the panes, and whose winds howled around the cathedral, making it seem inhabited by banshees. There were no afternoon or evening services scheduled today, so I felt quite alone, save these mysterious and distant wailings, which I reminded myself were not supernatural in nature, but simply the result of wind blowing through buttresses and across exterior statuary.

I was concentrating so hard that it was only when I had to squint to see through the glass and the first flash of distant lightning illuminated my perch that I realised it had got considerably darker, and much later. My watch informed me it was almost 5pm.

Crash! There was another fork of divine electricity, with its attendant rumble, as the gathering storm drew closer. I realised that it might not be sensible to be balancing so high above the ground in front of an electricity-conducting metal frame and began to climb down. In the next moment, my worry was vindicated. A terrifying blast landed on the cathedral's chancel, perhaps drawn by the conductor that stretched high above the tower. A finger of fire must have jumped between the metal pole and the window, for the many tormented faces of Christ lit up suddenly above me and a shattering occurred near the centre of the rose.

In fear, I fell from the ladder as shards of glass cascaded around me. Miraculously I landed upon a bundled groundsheet and suffered only bruised elbows and a slight graze to my left cheek. I turned my head, hearing the sound of footsteps running across the flagstones – archbishop Muncie and Fenton, the parson – then looked directly through a blue shard which had embedded itself in the wooden flooring an inch or two away from my face. A fraction closer and I might have been impaled!

As the archbishop began to ascend the spiral stairs, I found myself pulling this dagger of ancient glass free from the woodwork and secreting it in my inside pocket. There were a few other glass fragments scattered round and I picked myself up and began to gather these as the prelates approached. We all stood back to examine the rose, which had lost a section about as large as a man's forearm, a blue strip from Mary Magdalene's robe.

"Are you okay? We heard the crash. What on earth…?" began Muncie and it took five minutes for me to calm him and reassure him that I was unhurt and that the damage to the historic window was comparatively minor and could be repaired. I wound the remaining fragments in cloth, so that the archbishop would not notice a shard was missing. I wanted to examine the piece in my lodgings and didn't want to trouble him by asking permission.

I tried to refuse the archbishop's offer of hospitality, but he insisted on taking me to dinner in a private room in the adjacent public house, the Crooked Goose. I think he felt a little guilty that I'd come so close to calamity on his premises. He wanted to make amends with shepherd's pie and plum pudding. I took the opportunity, as we sipped our ales, to ask

Muncie about something that had been preying on my mind all afternoon.

"Your excellency..."

"Edwin, please," he admonished gently.

"Yes. Well, I've been meaning to ask you about something I encountered on my way to the cathedral. A gravestone, apparently near the side of a long-demolished house..."

"Lord John Hampton, the black lord," said Muncie, dolefully. "A regrettable part of our local heritage."

"Why black? He surely wasn't...?"

"Black in soul and spirit, Mr Pritchard. A man obsessed with the sins of others, and quite blind to his own. He became fascinated with the notion that witches covens were holding ceremonies in the woods hereabouts."

"This was in the seventeenth century?"

"That's right. In 1633, his mania came to a sordid conclusion. Having tried and failed to convince his household and the local worthies that there were such creatures at large, Lord John began to feel conspired against. It was said he was making regular sallies to a local house of ill-repute and became fixated with examining the bodies of the poor fallen women who resided there for signs of the devil – additional teats, numerals carved into their hindquarters, and suchlike. Eventually, it was said he was banished from the place and his obsession turned inwards, towards members of his own household. One foggy evening it's said he dragged his own maidservant out of her bed, tied her hands and took her down to the riverbank."

I couldn't believe what the prelate was telling me, aware that I'd been holding a forkful of pudding an inch from my mouth for almost a minute. I pushed the sweetmeat aside, agog at Muncie's tale, as he concluded.

"Lord John next summoned a gardener loyal to his cause. They threw a rope over the limb of a tree, suspended the poor maid by her wrists and dropped her into the icy torrent several times until she drowned, then left her corpse swinging in the wind. When the villagers heard of this atrocity, a group of them, including the murdered girl's parents came with torches and burned Hampton's home to the ground. Fortunately, his wife and three children escaped with their lives, but Hampton and two of his servants were trapped in an upper room and perished in the conflagration."

"Can this all really be true?" I said, astonished by the tale Muncie told, quite straightforwardly and with more embarrassment than emotion.

"It's all there in the annals of the parish beadle, if you care to take a look," Muncie muttered. "We ought to pull that stone down but some of the parishioners are superstitious and fear they'll be cursed if they remove it."

"Who placed it there?"

"His wife did, shortly before she left to lead a widow's life in Somerset, I believe the record holds. The day she left, the murdered maid's parents defaced it, removing all but a few traces of the rogue's name."

"And the girl?"

The archbishop frowned, then seemed to intuit my meaning. "Her name was Nancy Cartwright. Scarcely sixteen when she died. A senseless and stupid death."

I writhed among my sheets that evening, struggling to get to sleep in the remnants of the dissipating storm. The following morning, I rose late and missed Mr Eddington at breakfast. I decided to replicate my walk of the previous morning. In truth, I felt something drawing me towards that fateful location of despair, madness, and murder.

Despite the plentiful puddles the previous evening's storm had created, I made good progress and it was a little after 10am when I neared the brow of the hill where the decrepit fence had granted me access to the field. The rain had softened much of the ploughing and my shoes and trousers were soon soiled, but it scarcely mattered. Something was leading me inexorably down to the water's edge and that skeletal, supplicant tree.

Although a warmer morn than yesterday, still the sheltered bend of river at the base of the valley was swathed in mist once more. It never dissipates, I thought, then wondered why I held this certainty. I gingerly picked my way between the muddy runnels and down to the base of the twisted, broken-backed tree. I couldn't discern its variety and have no skill in horticulture, but it looked long dead, whatever it had once been.

I looked up and along the trunk, to see if I could find a limb overhanging the river. There! One such branch, as thick as a wrestler's thigh, reached out over the torrent, and there was something odd near its extremity – a circular depression in the bark, as if something had constricted its growth. Something like a rope?

Sir?

The voice, female, more of a whispering croak, issued from behind me. I whirled around, but there was nobody there. I felt suddenly cold, and pointlessly fearful. There had been nobody in the field but me, and no time for anyone to creep up unawares. Clearly my sleep deprived mind was playing tricks.

Mercy, goodly gentleman...

Again, the voice! Plainly now, constricted in pain or terror, this time on my other side, somewhere deep in the mist...

"Where are you?" I cried, hearing only my voice and the mocking chatter of crows.

I felt afraid now. Could it be? Was there something unnatural here with me, in this gloomy place? I remembered I still had the fragment of stained glass in my overcoat pocket.

Wrapping my handkerchief around its broad end, I drew it out as a dagger. A loose gleam of sunlight caught its blue surface and just for an instant I thought I saw a face there – a female visage, contorted…

No, it was surely my own, twisted in fear. I spun around, as a series of indistinct whispers rose, like a fugue of despair. Many voices… or one, somehow duplicated?

"What is this?" I cried. "What do you want?"

A creak from behind me, a repetitive sound… as of something swinging. I turned once more and there, suspended from the tree's stout limb, swathed in murky mist, was the indistinct figure I'd been dreading… a young woman, hanging.

Instinctively I held up my blade, clutching it so tightly that, despite my handkerchief, its edge, sheared by the lightning, sliced into my palm. The physical pain almost helped serve as a concrete distraction from the impossible apparition before me, from which I could not tear my gaze.

Release me, the voice seemed to hiss. What could it mean? I had no means…

The agonised form twisted in its agony, now writhing with heightened motion like a whirling zoetrope. I found myself beginning to climb the tree, the glass between my teeth like a savage. In moments I was out on that limb, fiercely hacking at the wood where the rope had cut deep into it. Had anyone seen me they'd have thought me as crazed as Lord Hampton. Not so crazy, in truth, because after a minute of stabbing at the wood, a final shriek went up and a heavy splash issued from below.

Droplets reached me at my perch, but the mist did not allow me to see anything drifting off down the river, and of course nothing could. I'd freed a shade, an incorporeal memory, and nothing more.

I jumped from the tree and ran from the field. Muttering to myself I staggered back towards the cathedral, still clutching the now bloody dagger derived from Mary Magdalene's skirts. On the path I met Mr Eddington, who'd managed to jar a couple of prime specimens of *bufo bufo* in the marshy wood nearby. He informed me later that I kept muttering the name of my beloved, Millie, and wouldn't be dissuaded from contacting her immediately. A telegram would not suffice.

Fortunately, the Tonbury Post Office had been supplied with a telephone just a few months prior and I managed to place a call through to an acquaintance, the Manager of the North British Hotel, which is only a short distance from our New Town flat. My friend kindly tolerated my rantings, then sent a porter running down to Randolph Crescent. There, our wonderful midwife Lettie was attending my beloved, who it appeared had just given birth, a full five weeks early, having suffered quite appalling pains in labour.

I felt immediately stricken by guilt that I was not there to witness the emergence of Harold Ignatius Pritchard into the world. I had not been an attendant husband lately, and Millie deserved better. I should be there with her now, I thought. I resolved to leave on the morning train – Tonbury Cathedral would have to wait for an answer to its mysteries.

Despite the expense of the call, I insisted Hettie put me through to Millie. Once I had her on the line, I finally handed off the bloody handkerchief and shard of blue glass to a concerned Mr Eddington, who quietly arranged for a physician to attend, once I relinquished the receiver. I told Millie I loved her and loved the child I'd not yet met. Apparently, our son was asleep at her breast and wore an expression of near-cherubic bliss. Millie was too pleased to hear from me to question my addled state of mind. I did not tell her what I had witnessed in that dismal valley.

Ten minutes later, as the local doctor crouched bandaging up my hand, I looked towards the sliver of glass that had set free a traumatised soul, and perhaps saved my own. I suddenly realised how oddly thin and smooth it appeared. Almost like glass from the sixteenth or perhaps seventeenth century.

"Eddington," I said, "do you know much about Black Lord Hampton and what became of the ruin of his home?"

Eddington was standing by the Post Office window, glancing through the mullioned pane. He seemed to be seeking inspiration in the sloping lane which led up towards the meadows.

"Yes. The landlord told me the tale last evening. I think the townsfolk pulled it down and scavenged what they could. It's said the old Tonbury wall contains some bricks taken from it, and I think some of the painted glass was recovered too."

"There was a stained window?"

"Oh yes, a seascape, quite fanciful. There's a painting of it in the town archive. I visited this morning. Fascinating place."

"And what became of this glass?"

He turned from the sunlit lane, smiling. "They don't waste anything, hereabouts. I believe some of it made its way into the windows of your cathedral."

The White Widow

I'm almost certainly the postman at the highest altitude in the British Isles, not a claim to fame I ever envisaged in my youth. Assynt's rocky trails, many of them eroded into a slurry of mud and gravel by autumn storms, are treacherous at the best of times, and the stretch I'm currently essaying, between Culnacraig and Dun Canna, is especially forbidding.

The fact that it's snowing heavily, and has been for several hours, should have given me pause. The woman who owns the guest house, at which I am the only resident, accosted me only this morning, armed with a pot of tea, scones, a sad shake of the head and the words, "Ah well, you'll no be wand'ring the postie's path the morin."

She said it as if it were a foregone conclusion, but I am adamantine when I've a scheme in mind and today would be no different. And so, belly filled at seven with a hearty cooked breakfast, then a second, entirely gratuitous second breakfast, I set off, with my Swiss walking poles, Arctic cagoul, woollen hat, heavy gloves, two pairs of socks and sensibly cleated footwear. I may be a little reckless, but I'm not entirely stupid.

My current mission began, as many such missions do, when I became irreparably lost on an obscure trail, one leading from the site of the prehistoric fort at Dun Canna northeast to the village of Strathcanaird. This occurred a month ago on the last trip I took with my wife Emily before she finally succumbed to that degenerate little tumour in her frontal lobe.

Emily sat sensibly ensconced by the fire in a local pub, reading, while I set out on what was to be my last trail run. I'd just turned seventy-two and my knees weren't up to the task of louping up rockfaces or shuddering down scree slopes. It had become too dangerous. Besides, even walking these remote Scottish outposts in one's fading decades is an act of exceptional optimism. The weather changes with fearful suddenness and fair becomes foul at the whim of the gods.

I'd made it four miles in, following the course of a burn. I was smugly glad I'd thought to wear plastic bags over my socks before putting on my hiking boots, a trick of my own invention. The boots were soddened from waterlogged stretches of peaty moorland, but my feet remained cosy. However, the rain progressed gradually from a misty smirr to a diagonal deluge. After an hour of this, having utterly lost the sheep path I'd been following, I began to have recurring fantasies of joining my wife in the Twa Corbies pub, whisky at hand, crackling fire warming my extremities. In that moment, my willpower broke, and I turned for home, immediately tripped over a rock and fell face-first into the heather.

The stumble didn't hurt or injure me, and nor was my pride much affected – I abandoned that luxury when old age began to render it redundant. Besides, there was nobody bar a few bedraggled sheep to notice my fall.

I turned to see what I'd tripped over, and there, half concealed by bracken, was a hewn stone, rather like a miniature headstone, or mile marker, its base firmly implanted in the soil. I pushed wet fronds aside to examine it. It was a piece of lichen-speckled granite, but it appeared to have indentations carved into one side. I looked closed and fancied I could make out the shape of a feminine face in profile, and a border of decorative swirls. It was a familiar shape but one that escaped my understanding until I made it back to the pub and recounted the incident to my wife.

"Ha!" she simply laughed once I'd finished my narrative. "Then you fared better than the last man who stumbled there."

What on earth was she talking about? I asked her to explain her cryptic utterance and she unfolded a strange story that made sinister sense of my wayward wanderings. It transpired she'd abandoned her novel for one of the books from the Corbies' own miniature library, mostly folklore, mawkish poetry, and local history. One of these texts had been entitled "Postal Paths and Drove roads of Assynt" by one Herbert B. Mannheim. The maps in the middle of this text had piqued her interest.

"It seems that once the penny post was initiated," Emily explained, "the local postal service received a flood of business. People began sending one another postcards, small gifts, love letters and other communications previously considered excessive. This created a problem of volume and efficiency for the postal office, which had to send horse and carriage along old military roads and overgrown drove paths. They decided to enlist a team of fit young men to shoulder backpacks full of correspondence and walk them over the more direct, but treacherous footpaths. They did this so efficiently, they'd sometimes beat carriages forced to take much longer routes."

Of course, quite frequently there would be accidents, and even deaths, Emily explained, her tone darkening. One such mishap befell a nineteen-year-old youth recruited to the postal service from Glasgow. He'd been teased by some of the local boys. They'd mentioned a grim spectre – a young, veiled woman who'd lead men astray. Although it was almost certainly simply an attempt to terrify this new recruit, one Hamish McAlpine, for cruel satisfaction, there was a link to local folklore, Emily revealed. Songs and poems told of a "white widow" who'd walk the hills and crags, and had the ability to transform into a seagull, a skirl of mist or even a sheet of windblown snow.

"She was widowed on the eve of her wedding, they say," Emily explained, "and hanged herself wearing her wedding dress. Folk think she wanders these lands searching for the shade of her fiancé, a farmer who'd perished in a terrible snowstorm."

"So, they scared this young postman with the story," I said. "What has that to do with my falling over in the heather?"

"The headstone," Emily said. "Some think it's there to honour the farmer who died, since it's right in the middle of his family's grazing land. The woman depicted is supposed to be his betrothed. But others say it's dedicated to Hamish McAlpine. You see, he never returned from his first foray out on the postal paths. His body was never found."

"But the carving on the stone…" I said and here Emily seemed to anticipate me, as she often did.

"It's a Penny Black."

Of course. That's why the image was so familiar – the young Victoria, ornately framed.

My grandfather's philately books I'd pored over as a child.

"That's astounding," I said, bending to kiss my wife on the forehead. There was an odd clamminess about her skin, despite her proximity to the fire. I should have sensed she'd be taken from me within weeks. We didn't spend nearly enough time together on that last trip, a regret I suspect will never leave me.

Emily had mentioned that there was a small collection of local antiquities in the village hall, so I waited out that wet weekend and then, at 10am on Monday morning, we both took a stroll to the small but sturdy stone building which contained a small meeting room, a low, curtained stage, and a couple of side rooms. One of these had a hand-written sign on its door, reading "Local Collections." The young woman who staffed the reception desk, Miss Finian, unlocked this door for us and led us through to a musty, damp-smelling library with a writing desk, a few church pews, a plan chest and three cases. Two were bookcases filled with old tomes too tedious to relate. The middle case, however, was a glass-fronted display of miscellaneous artefacts including Pictish jewellery, pieces of a Viking helmet and, oddest of all, an almost unmarked and empty envelope, bearing the remnants of a blob of sealing wax, but no stamp or postmark. The card beneath this last item read "Letter, found on the high path by Dun Canna, thought undelivered."

"Could that have belonged to Hamish McAlpine?" I couldn't help but wonder aloud.

"That it could!" came a stout voice from behind us, making me start. We turned and a reddish-faced man in his late forties there, rocking on his heels. He thrust out a meaty paw, which, after some hesitation, I shook.

"Geoff Truss," he said, as if his name explained something. "Local postman, and general busybody."

Over Truss's shoulder I saw miss Finian raise an arch eyebrow as she hovered solicitously.

"Are you the writers?" he beamed. I'd forgotten how fast word travels in such tiny communities.

"Well, I'm a writer. My wife's an academic."

Emily tutted. "And a writer too", she admonished, brushing her own hand against Truss's. "Though only if sixteenth century Italian poetry is your cup of tea."

Then she laughed in that generous, mellifluous way that never failed to melt my heart. Emily made everyone feel welcome and included. Moments later, she and Truss were fast friends, and we were sitting huddled like co-conspirators on a pew, discussing the history of the postal paths thereabouts which Truss, unsurprisingly, knew rather a lot about.

It was there, in that drafty village hall, and later, in the firelit lounge of the Corbies, that a strange plan developed. A scheme that I shared only with Emily. One I'm now enacting, here on this storm-scoured cliff-face.

The idea was so exciting, I called my editor immediately, pitching my idea for a semi-autobiographical account of wandering the postal paths of Assynt, carrying the last, undelivered letter of a young, tragically slain postman. Exactly the kind of thing the glossy supplement in question laps up. I had my commission within minutes. In fact, I was so carried away by both my own and my editor's enthusiasm that I entirely forgot to answer one vital question. How would I get hold of the letter?

Fortunately, once again, Emily solved my conundrum.

"Tell them you've arranged to have it DNA tested at my university, so they can know once and for all if it was handled by Hamish McAlpine. They've got bits of his uniform. It'll certainly have hairs or skin flakes. My colleagues in the genetics lab can run a quick check."

"Will they do that?"

"They will if I sweet-talk them. In the meantime, you can take it on your weird little pilgrimage, if it means so much to you."

I couldn't really explain it to her, but somehow it did. Emily fired off an email to a friend at the University, although we had to leave for Edinburgh before we got a reply. Before that happened, however, Emily's condition abruptly worsened, and she was hospitalised. She died just six days later.

After the funeral, and all the rigamarole around her last will and testament, I let my routine slide rather, until my son Gareth prompted me to shake myself out of my funk. I finally felt able to read my emails a week ago. I found three of immediate interest amongst the condolences, offers of assistance, and junk mail.

The first was from Emily's colleague's laboratory, confirming the booking for the document DNA check. The second was a gentle prompt from the magazine editor who wanted my Assynt piece. The third, however, was the clincher. It was from Emily.

She must have sent it a couple of days before she passed. I've no idea how, since I was at her bedside constantly, yet somehow my wife managed to cajole me from beyond the grave.

After relaying many fond reminiscences too painful to relate here, the letter ended with a curt command: do not mope! Then a single kiss and her familiar, ornate E-signature.

And that's why I'm here, tottering along this snow-blasted edge, where the contour lines seem to stumble over one another, and my feet are liable to do likewise. I'm a ridiculous old man, pursuing this perilous quest, and I'm probably going to end up the same way as the White Widow's fiancé and Hamish the novice postie, perishing here on a frozen nub overlooking the Atlantic.

I've lost the proper path to Culnacraig, and the slim runnel I'm following now is spotted with suspiciously large numbers of sheep droppings. The path veers away from the sheer edge of the cliffs, below which seabirds whirl, and heads uphill and inland, alongside a row of tormented trees. Too gnarly to identify, they resemble beseeching penitents, their hands stretched out towards a thin, V-shaped valley through which a burn tumbles. I make for it, noting that a similar blue vein is marked upon my map.

In my backpack there's an A4 document folder, inside which is a Ziplock bag containing the letter found near Dun Canna. Emily, Miss Finian, Truss, and I examined it with a magnifying glass before I carefully placed it between sheets of plastic and PVC. The name and address, oddly enough, were just visible, although the writing on the letter itself seems to have faded into insubstantiality.

"Perhaps written with a different pen, and less durable ink?" Miss Finian opined. Of course, we had no way of knowing if the single sheet of paper folded into quarters within the onionskin-thin envelope had ever contained writing. Perhaps some odd character had mailed a love token, such as a pressed flower, or a lock of hair, concealed within that vellum sheet, a sentimental trifle now lost to the ages.

What we did know was that the letter was addressed as follows:

The Lady in the Last House, by the Falls at Balwhinnie.

And that was all.

"Must be the row of abandoned crofts," Truss muttered, "There's bugger all of consequence there now."

I couldn't help but wonder, though. Was this letter addressed to the White Widow herself? Was it part of some elaborate prank by the postie's colleagues? On later examination, however, the timeline didn't work. Six months passed between the death of the betrothed crofters and young McAlpine setting out on his fateful journey. Whatever this message was would remain mysterious. I liked not knowing, I convinced myself – It would give me more to speculate about in my essay.

That is, if I ever reach my destination. The snow, which had consisted of thin, confetti like swirls, is now coming down in concentrated sheets, slicing across my path and eroding the very sheep-track I'm walking. There's an eerie silence to it – like a television channel detuned to static, with the sound turned all the way down. I feel winter's fingers penetrating my many layers, burrowing into the gap between scarf and coat, clasping at my ankles whenever my trouser leg rides up. Still, I press on.

I could hardly do otherwise. I estimate I've been walking for two and a half hours and am scarcely five miles into my walk, with two more to go. I look at my wristwatch, a gift from Emily, allowing icy flakes to caress my wrist for a moment. 2.55pm. At this time of year, it will be dark by four. I'd better hurry.

I begin to march, stiff-legged, chin pushed down onto my chest. This continues for agonizing, incalculable minutes. I hear a waterfall's tumult pierce the fearful silence. I look up and the path has vanished, although the valley's dark slash can still just be discerned through the white-out. Then something altogether stranger occurs.

The descending flakes seem to spiral together before me, perhaps simply in an eddying current of air. And yet for a fanciful moment, they seem to form a shape – a feminine form, arm outstretched, pointing… I rub my eyes; certain I'm delirious. I can't have seen a figure swathed in white, head shawled in some sort of… veil. This is perhaps the first indication of a dangerous chill. Can people experiencing the first signs of hypothermia hallucinate?

When I open my watery eyes, most of the form has vanished yet a head, shoulder and arm still float for a split-second, before dissolving on the wind. I follow the line of the spectre's finger. I see indications of a route, the merest suggestion of a path, a deeper channel of fresh snow among the hummocky heather. I march on, trying not to dwell upon what I've seen. Suggestion can be a marvellous thing and I've been thinking of little more than the White

Widow, and my Emily, for the last several hours.

I follow the possible path towards the waterfall's roar and there it is – half frozen into icicles, concealed and then revealed between granite slabs of shattered mountainside. My boots slip and slither, as I clamber among the wet rocks. And there, I finally spot what I've been looking out for – the remains of a cut stone, long and oblong and spotted with moss, but undeniably a lintel.

Around it, there are several piles of old stones, and fragments of long-rotten wood, indicating that a house once stood here, with its back to the falls and its face to the sea. Between cascade and ocean's roar, and certainly the last croft at Balwhinnie.

I duck behind a long, slanting slab which offers some respite from the blizzard. Shucking off my pack, I open it, unzip the document folder with shaking hands and extract the clear Ziplock bag. I'm not sure what I expect to happen, but I have an unaccountable craving to press the ancient letter against the lintel stone. I should not unzip the bag and take the paper out, I think, while finding myself doing exactly that.

A flash of the White Widow's spectral head, slowly turning to face me flickers into mind and I panic, picking at the paper as the wind catches it and whirls it out of my grasp.

"No!" I shout aloud, thinking of the trouble I'll provoke if I lose this precious local artefact. I run from my enclosure, leaping into deep snow and clutching for the spinning, teasing parchment. And of course, I fall there, tumbling helplessly as so many have before me. The farmer, McAlpine the postie, and now Benjamin Tulloch, writer, widower, hillwalker, and miscreant. I fall, and blackness comes rushing in, with the blizzard its veiled companion.

Two things stand out from the dream that soon pursues me. First, the unaccountable fragrance of mountain thyme, and secondly, a fragment of an old poem, one I'd read with Emily, by the freshly stoked fire of the Twa Corbies Inn.

I will twin thee a bow'r
By the clear silver fountain,
And I'll cover it o'er

Wi' the flooers o' the mountain
I will range through the wilds
And the deep glens sae dreary,
And return wi' their spoils
Tae the bow'r o' my dearie.

Will ye go, lassie go, I add, feeling an unaccountable warmth on both eyelids – a delicate kiss, such as Emily once bestowed.

I spasm back into consciousness, opening my eyes to see a sky darkening but thankfully free from icy petals spiralling down. I have no idea how long I've lain there, perhaps a couple of minutes, maybe more, before something woke me. I don't discover it until much later that day, but there's a small gash in my scalp, just under the hairline, but the blood has frozen stiff within my matted locks. My face and extremities feel oddly warm. I know this can't be a good thing, so I haul myself stiffly to my feet and look about me.

There is my backpack, half-covered in snow in the lee of the granite slab. And there, remarkably, just six feet away, is the letter, wet-through and wrapped like a lover's embrace around the lintel stone. I very gently peel it free and slip it back into the Ziplock bag. My watch reveals that I have only blacked out momentarily. That said, every minute counts on a Scottish winter's evening, so I grit my teeth, sling the backpack over my shoulder and begin to power up the rocky path I can now clearly discern crossing the top of the waterfall and continuing up and over the ridge.

A little under forty minutes later I reach Culnacraig, where a very worried Geoff Truss is waiting in his red Post Office van, having arranged to meet me there and drive me back to my guest house. I'd only told him about my plan to walk the postal routes alone; I'd shared nothing about the presence of the letter in my backpack.

"What kept you?" he jokes, relief flooding his features as he ushers me into the warm vehicle.

"Waylaid by the White Widow," I reply, as deadpan as I can muster, while wondering if what I've just jokingly suggested is in fact true. If I have encountered a phantasm, was she pointing to her long-destroyed domicile, or to the path to safety? Were her motives self-serving or charitable?

Three days later I'm back in Edinburgh and heading to a potentially futile rendezvous. I've carefully dried off the nineteenth century missive, in a takeaway box layered with muslin on top of a radiator turned down low. I'm now due to hand it over to Professor Sarah Hamlyn of the Historic Documents Department at Edinburgh University.

"What are you hoping to find out?" the surprisingly young yet sincere Professor asks me, almost as if I'm handing over a long-cherished family heirloom.

I sigh. "Oh, anything at all. Here's a couple of hairs from the postman who may have attempted to deliver the letter."

I hand over the tiny test tube that Miss Finian gave me, containing two tiny, twisted fibres which she assured me came from Hamish McAlpine's bunnet.

"Don't hope for too much," Professor Hamlyn cautions, "after this length of time, the chances of getting any live DNA are slim."

So it proves. I know from the regretful cast of Professor's head when I meet her in her departmental offices ten days later, that she's found nothing definitive.

"We can't say for certain who handled the letter and in fact, we couldn't even find evidence that anything had been written on it."

I nod, expecting as much. A disappointing end to a long-overdue article. My editor will not be pleased.

"Well, there was one odd thing," she adds, almost in consolation. "We detected the presence of some sort of herb, perhaps thyme? I might even speculate…"

Here Professor Hamlyn pauses, leaning in like a naughty schoolgirl.

"Well, it's possible that a love token, such as a sprig of mountain thyme, was enclosed. It was often a component of wedding favours, worn close to the bride's breast. Would that make any sense?"

I have an extraordinary and instant realisation, one accompanied by entirely unreasonable certainty.

The letter has nothing to do with my wayward postman at all. McAlpine might simply have found the letter on his wanderings that day, and felt compelled to deliver it, even months after the doomed farmer had addressed it. This would explain the absence of a stamp.

"It makes perfect sense, Professor," I reply, without elaborating. I somehow don't want to share my theory. It feels too… intimate.

Professor Hamlyn frowns slightly, the two tiny furrows on either side of her nose at the brow reminding me of Emily's quizzical expression when humouring me.

I suppose I will always be pursuing my own ghosts, after all, whether wandering snow scattered moorlands or simply dreaming. We are all walking fading trails with only one ultimate destination, after all.

Eyes in the Dark

I am not well-travelled, despite writing about places as far-flung as Indonesia and Svalbard. I'm an essayist and a novelist and when my now ex-wife asked me if I wouldn't rather hop on a plane than spend endless hours researching exotic places on the internet, I told her that's why God gave us imagination.

"But you don't believe in God," she said, mystified.

"That's right," I replied. "But I do believe in imagination. Lived experience is all very well but writing isn't just transcribing what we see, hear or feel."

In truth, I'm rather afraid of flying and I tend to get melancholy on holidays and trips abroad, particularly if I'm by myself. It's a love-hate relationship being an introvert. I'm both socially avoidant and morose when alone. Still, this gives me much to write about, solipsistic though my novels may be, as one critic recently pointed out.

When I was recently invited to Romania to visit and write about a newly discovered complex of karst caves containing prehistoric paintings which haven't seen the light of day for tens of thousands of years, I was both thrilled and filled with trepidation. My editor, too young and green to know any better, offered me this assignment because he'd read and loved my prehistoric thrillers, the Black Moon Trilogy.

Apart from one visit to the caves of Lascaux, I'd done all my research for those bestsellers in the British Library, British Museum, and online science journals. But Adam didn't know that, and he imagined an all-expenses trip to the Carpathian Mountains might both excite and inspire me. As much to save Adam's face as my own, I decided on this occasion to swallow my fears and counterfeit excitement for the upcoming trip.

My research assistant Tabitha, who to be honest had done most of the work behind the Black Moon books, couldn't be persuaded to come with me, and nor could my daughter who, I'll admit, I'd not previously spoken to for three months.

"Dad, I only live an hour away by train. You can't even be bothered to make that trip and you want me to use a week of my annual leave to come with you to Romania, of all places?"

Her scorn was withering and frankly unwarranted. I've had it in mind to visit her these last few months and if deadlines didn't keep reliably coming around to scupper my plans, I would definitely have gone to Winchester.

"Jane, at least talk to David about it, will you? Remember when we went to the caves at Lascaux?"

"I remember it rained incessantly and we had to queue in a downpour for a guided tour in German because you hadn't booked in time and the English one was full."

Jane sourly promised to talk to her husband, but I know she'd undersell the idea and I'd be travelling alone as usual. Two days later, Tabitha put me on a mercifully brief flight with a ghastly budget provider flying out of Luton. I vowed that this would be my last overseas commission, regardless of it being the cover story in Humanity, the magazine I most frequently write for.

For the first forty minutes of the flight, Andrei, the Romanian businessman sitting next to me, bored me with how much he loved London and how he hoped to grow his business renting chalets in the Romanian Alps to hunting parties. I told him I thought killing wild animals for sport was indefensibly cruel and the strategy worked quite nicely. Apart from the odd polite intrusion, I had the rest of the flight to myself and spent it re-reading The Brothers Karamazov.

Following the flight, I took a train from Cluj-Napoca to Brasov, a much more arduous journey, although the scenery was pretty enough. Nine hours with two changes of train, however. Surely Tabitha could have found a more direct route. When I finally stumbled into the four-star Excelsior Hotel in Brasov (it would be lucky to obtain three stars in London) I was thoroughly exhausted and elected to take a cold platter in my room rather than face a chattering restaurant. Tomorrow I'd meet Tatiana, the local cultural attaché, who'd be my guide to the caves. We'd be driving up there in her car and I confess I spent a restless night having oddly erotic fantasies involving my imagined sylph-like companion seducing me in the mountains.

In reality, Tatiana was pushing fifty, stout as a wrestler and clearly inclined more towards members of her own gender than mine. She had a very pleasing voice, however, and a smile of genuine warmth and professed herself a fan of my books. I felt we'd get on very well indeed. Her car turned out to be an old Rover TC2000, a vehicle not too dissimilar to one I'd owned in my youth. Tatiana was impressed that I recognised it, and we bonded over the pleasures and pains of owning a vintage motor car as we drove up winding 73 road towards the foothills of the Carpathians. The countryside was remarkably green and lush, with heavily forested regions interspersed with farmland and tiny villages. We passed a line of wagons, heavily laden with blue barrels of something or other, each vehicle drawn by two horses, dark-faced children scowling at us from the rear.

"Romanies," Tatiana explained needlessly. "They live like the nineteenth century."

What's wrong with that? I couldn't help but think but held my tongue.

"Do you like Bram Stoker?" said Tatiana, with a testing expression, like she was teasing me. A moment later, I realised why. We turned a corner and there on a rocky outcrop, surrounded by forest, was an impressive castle, its steep stone sides, and turreted roofs immediately familiar. With a flush of embarrassment, I realised this must be Bran Castle. Why hadn't I known it would be on our route?

"Of course. Count Dracula's supposed home. It rather lives up to the hype."

"Glad you like," said Tatiana, raising an eyebrow. "Was closed to tourists a couple of years ago. Too dangerous. Do you know why?"

I thought for a moment and shook my head.

"Family of brown bears moved in," she said. "You don't mess with bears."

I laughed a little uneasily, realising we were about to drive deep into the forest in a fifty-year-old car that had probably already had its fair share of breakdowns.

"How, er, far is our hotel?"

Tatiana laughed. "Hotel it is? Lodge is thirty-two miles into mountains. Hold onto your hat, Mr Buckhurst. May be a bumpy ride."

An astonishing two and a half hours later, as the sun was skimming the tops of the trees, we were still rollercoasting up and down narrow roads whose left-hand sides were pitted with massive potholes.

"Why are the roads ruined on one side only?" I asked Tatiana.

"Logging," she replied, leaving me to work out the implication by myself. I guessed that full logging trucks roaring down the mountainside caused most of the damage whilst the empty ones on our side were far less destructive. I felt rather pleased with myself, as my theory was proven by one of those monstrous eighteen wheelers roaring by at unconscionable speed as we swerved onto the verge to avoid a collision. The driver's air-horn blast either signified mania or some species of apology. Probably the former, since most Romanians, Tatiana included, seem to drive like maniacs.

We almost missed the turning, a tiny gravel track forking away from the main road alongside a rushing stream. Tatiana reversed at speed and righted her route, revealing that this was only the second time she'd come here, the first being to bring the team of archaeologists and palaeontologists who had spent a month here cataloguing, photographing, and measuring everything.

Apparently, the site had been discovered when logging and weather erosion caused a landslide, opening up the mouth of a thirty-foot-long limestone cave, and a habitation not seen for perhaps fifty thousand years. The very thought of it sent a shiver down my spine. In spite of all my misgivings, I was looking forward to being only the tenth person to see the cave paintings since humans first explored the Eurasian continent.

It was too dark to see much by the time we arrived at the small, prefabricated shelter that Tatiana had termed a "lodge". That turned out to be a rather grandiose term for what was really a glorified bothy. It had a communal room and two bedrooms, each containing four bunk beds.

Each room had a wood-fired stove for heating, a rudimentary shower, and a toilet. Laminated instructions in broken English revealed that you had to keep the stove going for half an hour in the main room before the water would be warm enough to shower. I decided to give this a miss until tomorrow.

The communal room boasted a range to cook upon, a pile of cut logs, plus cupboard space, tables, and chairs. The windows rattled in the growling wind and a sudden hailstorm gave us both a start as Tatiana fuelled and lit the fire. I had to admit that my guide was both resourceful and thoughtful. However, it was bitterly cold and draughty in the wooden shack. Fortunately, there were piles of clean blankets, so we helped ourselves to several each and after a reheated bowl of Tatiana's unspecified meat "stew", said our fatigued good nights and went to our respective bunkrooms. It was scarcely nine pm, but I felt thoroughly drained by my journey. Late autumn had so far proven reasonably mild, but the weather could change suddenly at this time of year at this altitude, Tatiana informed me. I put an extra pair of socks on and read a few pages of Dostoyevsky by torchlight before giving in to my exhaustion.

That night, although I slept surprisingly soundly, I was troubled by a strange and ambiguous dream. I found myself in a forest clearing, for some reason attempting to replace the tyre on a logging truck (quite unlike me, if you knew anything about my level of vehicular expertise). Nevertheless, I had got the damaged tyre free and was about to roll a fresh one into place when a hunched, bedraggled figure burst into the clearing.

He was scarcely five feet in height and had the prognathous jaw, bulbous forehead, and flattened nose of some species of prehistoric humanoid, whether neanderthal or homo something-or-other, I couldn't say. He wore a loose-fitting loincloth of hide and his muscular body was thickly matted with dark hair, which was smeared in places with something darkly red, presumably blood. As I froze in place, half-hidden by the cab of the truck, the creature sniffed the air, seeming to search for the source of something. I held my breath, hoping that something wasn't me.

The creature suddenly met my gaze, turning his head to one side, like a dog does when he's trying to understand his master. I froze in fear as the humanoid hoisted a flint-pointed spear aloft and nimbly dashed across the gap between us. I flinched and threw up my arms but found myself frozen to the spot as the humanoid pulled one shoulder back, preparing to hurl the spear. I could almost anticipate the searing pain of that blade, imagining it tearing through my chest. My attacker unleashed a cry both animalistic and filled with inchoate rage.

I awoke sweating, entangled in my blankets, and lay in my top bunk, afraid to move for a moment until I remembered where I was. Hopefully, I had not cried out, as I sometimes do when dreaming. It would be a significant embarrassment to be discovered in my babyish fears by Tatiana. Eventually I was able to turn my head and see the empty, moonlit room, with just the dull red glow of the stove's embers to provide human warmth.

I did not sleep further that night, pacing the room to keep warm at first, then going into the adjoining main room to light the range for hot water. I impressed myself by accomplishing this within ten minutes using the remains of an old newspaper and several logs. By the time Tatiana appeared, I'd even managed to make a pot of coffee on the range. My guide's raised eyebrow revealed that I had exceeded her somewhat inadequate assessment of me.

Ninety minutes later, we were fed, showered, dressed, and picking our way up the winding trail hacked out by loggers who had gone to investigate the landslide, then further flattened by the scientists who had followed. It was a twenty-minute walk and involved much clambering over fallen trees and edging around precipitous slopes. Fortunately, I'd bought a new pair of hiking boots for the trip and they stood me in good stead.

Nevertheless, I was rather out of breath and light-headed when we arrived at the cave mouth. Somewhat annoyingly, Tatiana seemed to be entirely untroubled by the exertion.

A long tangle of fallen trees, dirt and rocks had fallen away to reveal a vertical slash in the limestone bluff. Evidently a layer of rock had sheared off when the slope collapsed, since the exposed rock was free from lichen and vegetation. The cave mouth resembled an obscenely grimacing mouth turned on its side. The interior was utterly dark, in contrast to the grey-green limestone surrounding the entrance. We switched on our hand torches and crept into the gloom.

Before we turned our attention to the walls, Tatiana's mission was to locate the generator and working lights the scientists had left behind for future use. She accomplished this with ease and moments later a chugging oil-fired machine supplied enough electricity to light up four large klieg lights and throw the interior of the cave into sharp relief.

The space was bottle-shaped, the neck tapering off into the far side of the cave and ending in darkness. Tatiana had informed me that a second cave might lie that way, but the bottleneck had been filled in with rubble. Further explorations would ensue in the spring.

I stepped back from the widest wall, to the left of the entrance behind me, and felt my heartrate rise as before me spread a canvas of ancient drama – a herd or bison-like animals, with smaller deer-like shapes, pursued by a small army of stick figures. Swirls and spirals of dots decorated the scene, and the colours were still remarkably vivid – a dark red like congealed blood, a yellowish ochre, and an ashen blue-grey. The stick figures and animals were outlined in black, probably with charcoal. The entire frieze was full of life and it was hard to grasp that it may have been painted tens of thousands of years before.

"Turn around," said Tatiana softly, "the artists left self-portraits."

I spun around and Tatiana had swivelled one of the lights to illuminate the more knobbly, sloping opposite wall of the cave. Arcing all the way up from floor to ceiling was a zig-zagging pattern of interlocking handprints. They looked stencilled on, the pigment outlining the hands smeared evenly and fading gently into the naked stone as if airbrushed.

"It's believed they blew the paint from their mouths," Tatiana says and suddenly I saw the scene. More specifically, I saw the creature from my dream leaning against the wall, mouth filled with berry juice, spraying liquid against his outstretched hand. The handprints were smaller than my own; I couldn't help but stretch out my left palm to place it over one of them, realising moments later that I perhaps should have asked for permission first.

"It's okay, everyone does it," Tatiana said, answering my unasked question.

The handprints were not all uniformly small, although they were all smaller than my own would be. There were some tinier outlines, near the floor, presumably the prints of children. The sight of these tiny, familiar shapes brought a lump to my throat and I quashed the memories that started to form. Jane lay asleep in my arms in the hospital still clutching my finger, even in sleep. I wasn't about to cry in front of the Romanian cultural attaché, so I pulled myself together and took off my backpack to retrieve my sketch book and pencils.

"I arrange for a couple of scientists to come and visit tomorrow but I want you to see it… pure," said Tatiana, reaching for the word. Uninflected, I thought, without offering the clarification.

I'm a reasonably accomplished sketch artist, and I wanted a record more personal and tactile than a mere photo, so I unfolded a canvas stool and sat down to draw the hunting scene. Within seconds, I became so engrossed I almost completely forgot that Tatiana was still there.

"I have some provisions to buy," she suddenly announced. "We will need more firewood too. I'll get in town. Are you okay if I leave you for an hour or so?"

I was a little disappointed that she wasn't intending to chop the logs herself with a mighty axe and could picture the scene vividly. Evidently middle-class conveniences had reached even rural Romania. I nodded and returned her smile, then went back to my drawing.

Shortly, I heard the distant wheeze and splutter that announced the Rover's engine starting, down in the valley below. I could see her car pull away from the lodge, which could just be made out through the thinning pines.

It was getting a little chilly as I munched on the packed-lunch I brought with me and drank coffee from the flask. The drawings would take some time. It felt important to capture the sense of fluid action in the scene before me. I wondered just where the tribesmen were herding the animals, and why. Was this an illustration of persistence hunting, whereby hunters wore down the fleet-footed animals until one or more of them dropped through exhaustion? I would ask this and other questions of the scientists I'd meet the following day.

I felt a little odd sitting with my back to the wall of handprints, almost as if hands might emerge from that strangely domestic frieze and grab me. I knew I was being fanciful, however, and shrugged away my fears. What I really wanted to do was light a fire. For one thing, it was getting rather cold and the wind was building to fury again beyond the cave-mouth, howling drafts penetrating the interior to where I sat.

Secondly, I really wanted to see these paintings the way their creators would have. I'd read that they really came alive and even seemed animated in the flickering flames of a hearth. Would it be so awfully bad to light a small fire here now? I guessed that I probably shouldn't, in case the smoke damaged the frescoes, but as soon as I had this thought it seemed ridiculous. These walls had been lit up by firelight and patinaed by woodsmoke for centuries. There were actually the remains of a fire here in any case, presumably made by the loggers who first found the cave, as well as a pile of unburnt tangled branches and logs.

In the end, after who knows how long, the oil-fired generator made my decision for me, together with the gathering storm. Two things happened in quick succession. First, I realised it had grown quite dark beyond the vertical slash of the cave entrance. I glanced at my watch. It was almost 4pm. I'd been drawing for three hours. Oddly, I'd hardly felt the time pass, although my frozen knuckles and stiff legs testified to how long I'd been sitting for. I walked to the cave mouth and was buffeted by a gust of wet wind that scoured my face viciously. A full storm was raging outside, and I'd somehow been entirely oblivious!

The trail was already being eroded by rivulets of rainwater and I couldn't see any sign of

Tatiana's car down in the valley below. If I'd had any phone signal, I'd have called her but surrounded by granite and limestone mountains on three sides, there wasn't so much as a flicker of reception on my outmoded Nokia.

I decided to try my luck with the trail, reckoning I'd be safer and more comfortable in the lodge than the cave. However, after one too many disastrous and painful slips, the last of them sending me toppling towards the lip of an abyss, I realised it was now too dark and dangerous to attempt the path, even with a torch. I returned to the cave to wait out the storm, or Tatiana's return.

The second calamity which befell me was that the generator, whose oil reservoir must have been perilously low when we arrived, began to splutter, the Klieg lights flickering decisively. I tilted the generator to encourage the remaining oil to flow into the combustion chamber, or whatever it was called, but I doubted I had more than a few minutes of electricity left. That realisation clinched it. I grabbed handfuls of twigs and dry bracken and began to build a fire in the blackened space in the centre of the cave, lifting the lights closer to the walls to give me space to work.

I decided to sacrifice a few of the remaining pages of my sketchbook and was glad to discover that I pocketed the lighter I used to light the stove this morning. Just as the generator wheezed to a halt and the lights went out, I managed to get the paper to catch and the smaller twigs followed suit. Within ten minutes, the cave was illuminated with the amber flickering of a roaring fire. I felt a sense of pride in my second act of fire-lighting that day, which momentarily overcame the primitive fears lurking at the back of my mind, somewhere in the basal ganglia where the nightmares lived.

I realised I was wet through and there seemed no reason to remain modest, given the circumstances, so I stripped off and hung my shirt, trousers, jersey, and coat over the light stands, so that they caught the fire's heat. They would be dry in no time and although everything would stink of woodsmoke, at least I wouldn't perish from pneumonia. I was conscious of my flabby belly as I stood up in my socks and walked to the cavemouth, edging along one wall to stay out of the rain as it slanted down. I could dimly make out the streetlamps and illuminated windows of a village on the opposite hillside and the taillights of a few vehicles winding their way around distant B-roads, but there was no sign of life from our valley. Something must have happened to Tatiana. An accident, a flooded track, or a mudslide, perhaps a tree fallen across the road. It could be any of these things. Perhaps the likeliest explanation was the Rover having broken down; I regretted having cooed over the ancient automobile quite so much.

I returned to the fireside and positioned my backpack to create a pillow, then spread out some of the dried bracken that littered the cave floor. I might just rest awhile, I thought. Perhaps a little lie down to recuperate from my ordeals. As I lay my head down, I looked up at the dancing, panic-stricken animals fleeing their hunters. The antelope seemed to be leaping over the little diamonds of flame that separated from the main mass of the conflagration. The crackle and scent of burning pine began to have something of a soporific effect. I wasn't planning to fall asleep, just rest my eyes awhile...

I woke with a start; the flames having died down considerably. I had the unmistakable sensation of being watched. Again, I felt the prickling along the arms and the back of the neck. I was afraid to turn, for I knew who would be there. I was an interloper in his domain. There was a strange sound, like something sniffing and I felt hot breath upon my neck. I could have turned round, and confirmed my terrors but I was surely fantasising, so instead I lay back down, closing my eyes firmly. My body curled in on itself, refusing to turn and confirm my trespass upon the creature's domain. Somehow, even though my eyes were firmly closed, out of the darkness of the cavern behind my eyes rose a pair of startlingly intelligent blue eyes, pushing forward into pale illumination to reveal a high eyebrow ridge, matted hair and then a curl of jutting top lip that revealed a cruelly curved incisor.

I woke again... this time for real, revealing my previous experience to have been a dream. I was almost naked and shivering, with the dull, pinkish embers of the fire revealing that I had been asleep for hours. My watch did not have an illuminated dial, but I guessed it read a little after 11pm. Disaster must have befallen Tatiana, and I wase quite alone.

As I reached out for my shirt, I heard it. Something not quite human. A deep-throated grumbling sound. Something waking, something lying in the shadows of the bottleneck of the cavern. It raised its head and I made out thick black fur, a snout and, in the dim moonlight and reddish fire's afterglow, the incisors from my dream. But this was no imagined neanderthal. This was a very real brown bear. One that had no doubt also sought refuge from the storm in this warm cave, perhaps not even noticing my presence until now.

My heart was beating a crazed tattoo as I desperately tried to remember what advice Tatiana gave me about encountering a bear. I think it amounted to little more than don't. Bears can run faster than a man, climb trees and swim rivers. If a bear wants to take you down, it probably will, was the general message I got from the cultural attaché.

I shrank back against the wall, willing my half-asleep legs into utility. I needed to get out of there, and fast. Potentially without my clothes, if that what it would take. The animal gradually rose onto all fours, then pushed itself onto its hind legs, almost like a man arising from a sound slumber. If I had awoken this animal from the start of its winter hibernation, that didn't bode well for its congeniality.

I had the embers at my back and the bear in front of me. I slunk into the shadows of the wall and started to back away as the beast reared up to its full height and roared at me. The noise was terrifying, even without the echoes of the cave extending its life. I felt a gust of hot, moist breath engulf me as the bear lolloped out of its corner. I backed further away at speed, wondering if I should roar back, when I felt something hard and metallic collide with my back. One of the lighting stands toppled over, its lamp hitting the stone floor of the cavern, the bulb exploding. Glass showered my feet.

The bear roared again and swiped at me with one immense paw as I tried to scramble away. A sensation like a garden rake slamming into my chest spun me round, bouncing me off the wall and directly onto the still-hot embers of the fire. I screamed and scrabbled out of the ashes. The bear hesitated, uncertain whether to move in for the kill or let me escape. Then, as I scrambled out of the cinders, I felt, rather than saw it lurch forward again, and everything slowed to a crawl, as one might imagine one's last moments doing.

Turning my head and damaged chest away from my attacker I saw a pair of bright and intelligent eyes in the darkness of the cavemouth. Then a mouth opened, white with tiny sharp teeth. A chest thick with matted hair, splattered red. I felt a shock of recognition as the newcomer first turned its head to one side, then placed a finger to its lips, in the universal sign for silence. I felt myself freeze, like I had in my dream. What would be, would be.

The thick lips pursed and blew, and an immense blast hit both me and the fire's embers. Flame leapt into being and the bear backed away in fear, whimpering. I had screwed my eyes shut but now opened them to see nothing before me but the open cavemouth. I grabbed my coat from the floor and ran out into the now-dwindling storm, pressing the bundled fabric against my torn chest as I slipped and scrambled down the trail and back to the lodge.

I have no idea how long I lay bleeding and half-delirious, wrapped in blankets on the floor of the main room. At some point a vehicle drew up and two men carried me out into a waiting Jeep. I believe Tatiana was with them but by this point I had lost a lot of blood and nothing cohered – neither my thoughts, my sense impression, or my perception of time itself. I remember vaguely bumping down the gravel track and then an injection being applied to my forearm. I remember the taillights of the Rover as our vehicle followed it down onto blessed tarmac once more.

My recovery was slow and filled with troublesome half-memories and nightmares. I could hardly tell fact from feverish fiction and was unable to separate the bear in the cave from my memory of the apparition who had apparently saved me. The bear's claws had raked me down to the ribs. When I awoke blood was seeping through my bandaged chest from hastily applied stitches. Fortunately, after a couple of calls, Tabitha and Tatiana arranged my convalescence and the necessary insurance. "How do you feel?" was the first sentence from Tatiana I felt able to process when I awoke on the fourth morning after my ordeal.

"Confused...", I replied, "and dehydrated." Tatiana poured me water and listened to my chaotic, scarcely credible story. I described the bear in full detail but, for some reason, felt unable to mention the humanoid who had saved me from its clutches. Once Tatiana had listened to my recap, she very calmly explained what had happened to her and confirmed certain aspects of my own story.

"I broke down halfway up the gravel track. Could not get car started," she began. "I decided to walk back to the village to get help. But the storm was ferocious so I stayed there, imagining you must have gone to lodge. I would send mechanic in morning to fix car and collect you. When storm started dying down, I met Yuri and Alexandr and we decided to take Jeep to check on you."

"Thank you. I might have…" I replied feebly. "Well, thanks. But… the bear?"

"We see droppings and footprints," she said. "Brown bear… and… human ones."

I attempted a laugh, but it became a grimace of pain.

"I took off my wet clothes and my shoes."

"And socks too?"

"No, I was never barefoot."

Tatiana frowned slightly. "That's odd. Did you fall in the fire?"

She had not criticised me for building a fire and had in fact agreed that it was the right decision. People die from exposure in the Carpathians at this time of year.

"I did. Trying to get away from the bear. Fortunately, it had all but gone out."

"You will have big scar, I think," she said, looking more than a little apologetic. I suspect her bosses at the Department of Culture might have given her a dressing down for leaving me alone in a gathering storm. Strangely, I felt no animosity towards my guide. I had wanted to be alone with the elements and the ancient artworks. I had longed for solitude to ingest all that was ancient and unknowable. I had got more than I'd bargained for. I vowed to write to Tatiana's superiors in support of her hospitality and quick thinking. I would certainly have perished on the mountainside had she not returned for me.

I called Jane from the hospital to let her know what was happening, since she had expected an update regarding my trip. At least, I'd assumed she'd expected a call. Her first words to me were "Dad? Two calls in one month. You're spoiling me." Jane changed her tone immediately when I told her about the cave, the storm, and the bear. I did not talk about the apparition.

I had all but decided that my neanderthal saviour was a full figment of my frenzied imagination, a being constructed from pure panic and adrenalin, when something happened that threw me back into incomprehension. It was on the seventh day of my recovery, when I came to remove my bandages in the local hospital's surgical ward, so that the duty doctor could examine my stitches. A full-length mirror was positioned in the curtained off cubicle and I was left alone while a fresh bandage was sourced. I stood before the tall glass and examined my tortured body. I had three livid, diagonal slashes across my ribcage and a sequence of smudgy bruises testifying to the many falls I'd suffered scrambling down the trail.

But what most perplexed me was the red-black weal on the small of my back. Looked at from one angle, it could clearly be interpreted as the burnt imprint of coals from the fire. But viewed from my own vantage-point it resembled nothing more nor less than the outline of a diminutive hand, placed there in support, or perhaps as a vivid warning against trespassing the incalculable ages.

The 7 Sampler Series

About the Author

Gavin Boyter is a Scottish writer now living in Margate, Kent. Having previously worked in advertising and healthcare, he is now concentrating on creative writing and freelance copywriting. In 2018, he ran from Paris to Istanbul, as described in his 2020 book *Running the Orient*. Boyter is also a screenwriter with two optioned projects in development, including the psychological thrillers *Nitrate* (co-written with Guy Ducker) and *20 Questions*.

A documentary film version of Boyter's first running book, *Downhill From Here*, is in the works. In 2021 he released his first collection of short stories, *Running Coyote and Fallen Star* and in 2023 published the crime novel *Elena in Exile*.

Boyter loves running long distances, wild swimming, and will almost certainly never learn to play the guitar properly.

Other Books by Gavin Boyter:

Non-Fiction

Downhill From Here
Running the Orient
Run for the Hell of It

Fiction

Running Coyote and Fallen Star
Elena in Exile

www.gavinboyter.com